the magic of death

dead end witches
book one

Leslie Gail

For Tor
...and beyond!

chapter
one

GRANNY SAYS there's nothing more valuable in this world than family, but at that moment I would've traded every single one of them for just a few more minutes of sleep. I shot a glance over my shoulder at my bed and imagined crawling back in and pulling the covers over my head. Instead, I dumped out the contents of my ceramic Tardis trinket box. The various name tags in assorted shapes and hues spilled out across the smooth oak surface of my dresser. I grabbed the one shaped like a coffee cup, wishing it was an actual cup of coffee, and pinned it to my apron.

I would have to get used to very little sleep for the rest of the month because October in Dead End was like summer at the beach; bodies littering every available inch of space. And that weekend—the opening weekend of Dead Fest—was the kickoff to the season. I'd be working in most, if not all, of the various family businesses that week, so to save myself time later, I shoved all the name tags into my apron pocket, along with my amulet, and secured my unruly auburn hair with a scrunchy. My hair was both curly and wavy, as if it didn't really know what it wanted to be when it grew up. Kinda like me. Which might be why I allowed my relatives to use me as cheap labor instead of starting something of my own.

I tiptoed down the creaky wooden stairs so I wouldn't wake Teeny and Aunt Merilee. And possibly Uncle Gavin. He's Aunt Merilee's—at least on paper—husband. I didn't know whether he was still downstairs in Aunt Merilee's bed or if he'd already snuck out like he usually did, but the only people they were fooling were themselves. They've been married for decades and split up before the ink was dry on the marriage license—as the story goes—but never bothered to get officially divorced. They had this on again-off again thing going they thought was a big secret. Spoiler alert: it wasn't.

I grabbed my schedule off the fridge, shoved it into my purse, and glanced at the dried goop on the stove— probably pancake batter—that my niece Teeny had missed while cleaning the kitchen the previous night. She was usually rather good at helping around the house, but she hadn't been herself for the past few weeks. She'd insisted nothing was wrong, but she'd gotten detention for getting into a screaming match with another student the day before. Aunt Mer frequently reminded me that Astra and I were a handful at that age as well, but this felt like something more than normal angsty teen years. If only I could talk to Astra about it. But as she'd abandoned me twice—once by leaving me in life and once in death—I'd have to figure it out on my own.

"Good morning, Star," Caroline called from her usual spot in the tree next to the driveway. I assumed it was her because despite common lore, ghosts don't actually glow in the dark. They look just like you and me except they shimmer slightly—like a hologram—but you have to look close to see it. And yeah, if you guessed it had caused some pretty awkward situations over the years, you'd be right. On days I didn't want to deal with it, I wore the amulet Granny had made me years ago.

"You'll never believe who I saw last night near Merilee's bedroom window," she said.

I bet I could. I climbed into the Jeep and turned the key.

"Have a nice day, hon!" she hollered loud enough to wake not only our house, but the neighbors a few acres away. Fortunately—for the sake of everyone's sleep—I was the only one who could hear and communicate with the many spirits around Dead End.

But that didn't mean I had to talk back to them. I retrieved the amulet from my pocket and fastened it around my neck and Caroline disappeared like grape jelly meatballs at a potluck.

I drove through the winding country roads while listening to my latest audio book and pulled into the parking lot of my younger cousin Holly's breakfast only restaurant—Mourning Brew—less than fifteen minutes later. The tourists seem to love the punny names, but I swore if I ever had my own business, I would name it something less cheesy.

Dead End hadn't always been a tourist town. It was once just another small sleepy Central Texas town with a population of nine-hundred and seventy-two people. The base hadn't changed much, but tourists descended like locusts every October. You can blame my youngest sister, Daisy, for this madness. Once she became a viral internet star, got her own ghost hunting show, and mentioned her hometown—the one she lived in for just a few years and got out of as soon as she could—everything exploded around here.

I shouldn't complain because the tourists keep us in business. However, they brought along other sorts of problems too. More litter, more traffic, and fewer parking spaces. At least that was one good thing about having to get up so early on the days I worked at Mourning Brew— plenty of spots for me to choose from.

"Sorry, I'm late!" I called through the back door.

I nearly bumped into Sheri, one of Holly's employees, who was filling the baking racks with clean trays. Holly wore headphones over her blonde bob and moved her head to the beat coming through them. And while she was five feet three to my five feet eight she had the presence of someone you didn't want to mess with. And not just because she was holding a butcher knife that looked as if it could be used in a beheading. I made a wide arc around her so she could see me before I spoke to her.

She removed her headphones and let them rest around her neck. "Hey, Star! What are you doing here?"

"Sorry I'm late," I repeated. "I had a rough night! But I'm here and ready to work."

"You're not scheduled until ten today. Deb and Sheri are here for the early morning shift." As if on cue, Deb stepped out of the freezer with more butter and waved.

I waved back and strode to the dry erase board where our schedule was secured with a magnet. She was right. I'd gotten out of bed at three thirty for nothing. I rested my forehead against the wall.

Holly placed her knife on the stainless-steel table and crossed the room. "You okay, hon?"

"Just exhausted."

She pointed to the extra chair next to her desk. "Sit. Sheri, can you get Star a cup of coffee, please?"

Sheri nodded and disappeared through the swinging doors.

"You're working much too hard," Holly laid a hand on my knee.

I worked hard, but my exhaustion had just as much to do with my nightmares as my daytime activities. But broaching that subject would lead to another subject—dead sister who refused to speak to me. And I didn't want to talk about it.

"Should I fire you so you can get some rest?" Holly stared up at me earnestly.

"No, I love working here. I mean, the hours are insane, but the tips are good. Plus, free biscuits are the best employee benefit I could ask for." I grinned.

"You know can have free biscuits anytime you want, but excellent answer. I enjoy having you around." She shoulder-bumped me. "So, what about quitting The Merc?"

The Mercantile—which we in the family all just called The Merc but was recently renamed Toil and Trouble for the tourists—was the eclectic shop my grandmother owned. She did tarot card readings upstairs in the living room of her apartment, and I ran the shop downstairs when she needed me to.

"Are you kidding? You know Granny won't hire anyone else. She says four employees are enough. And she's counting herself and Aunt Tatty in that number."

Holly made a face that showed the frustration I felt. "But Granny can't get down the stairs like she used to."

"Exactly! And with Gayla back in college now, that just leaves me and Aunt Tatty. And Aunt Tatty would rather prance naked down main street than do any actual work."

Holly groaned and placed the heel of her palms over her closed eyelids. "I'm gonna have to stab myself in the eyeballs to remove that terrifying image from my head."

I squeezed my eyes shut. "Yeah, I'm not so proud of that one myself, since I have a horrifying image in my own head."

"What about quitting Pub Dead?"

"I'm only there a couple of nights a week and the Monday night trivia crowd gives the best tips. Even better than here. It's just until Boone is back. Besides, it's the only night Aunt Merilee and Uncle Gavin can have some non-sneaking-around alone time since Teeny's usually at volleyball practice or some other activity."

"They're still acting like we don't all know they're back together?" Holly shook her head but smiled.

"Yeah. He came over last night to fix the hot water heater, but after he finished, Aunt Mer said he may as well stay for dinner because her Mamma would skin her alive if she sent him home hungry."

"As if she's ever been afraid of Granny!" Holly shook her head.

"Right?! Dinner led to movie night and after it ended, Uncle Gavin hugged me and Teeny bye, nodded to Aunt

Mer, then climbed into his truck and left. Aunt Mer immediately made a big deal of yawning and stretching and saying how exhausted she was, and she all but ran to her room."

"Oh my gosh, they're worse than teenagers!" Holly chuckled.

"For sure, and much less discreet. Less than half an hour later, I saw the beam of his flashlight bobbing in the yard, then heard a noise that sounded like he fell through Aunt Mer's bedroom window and took her bedside lamp down with him. But the racket she made shushing him was even louder than his tumble to the floor." I rolled my eyes but smiled. Aunt Mer deserved a bit of happiness.

Sheri placed a hot cup of coffee in my hands. "Neither of them is married. Why don't they just make it public?"

"I think that's the point. I honestly believe if they didn't have to sneak around, they'd most likely break up again." I sipped the hot liquid and felt myself come to life.

Sheri shook her head. "You Bells are such complicated folks."

"You don't even know," said Holly. Then she turned back to me. "Hey, you got me off the subject."

"Of?"

"Getting you to cut back on one of your many jobs. Where else are you working these days?"

"I think that's about it. It's the end of the growing season, so Aunt Mer only needs me at the greenhouse occasionally. Isaac has some local high school kids helping him after school at the ice cream shop, so he's mostly covered there. Oh, but I've promised your Mamma I'd put out more campaign signs around town."

"Star! Learn to say no. You have your hands full."

"No, it's fine! Really. Besides, I want your Mamma to win."

"I do too, but when do you sleep?"

"Here and there." I shrugged. I'd rather work than close my eyes and dream of Astra.

"The family can survive without your help. You're going to exhaust yourself into a coma. If you weren't so tired, you wouldn't have gotten your schedule mixed up. Why don't you go back home and get a few hours of sleep?"

"I'd rather just stay here and make biscuits. I don't want to run into Uncle Gavin sneaking into the kitchen in his underwear for a glass of water."

"Fine, but you have got to stop with the visuals, girl!" Holly stood and shoved her headphones back on.

A few hours later, I'd served enough biscuits and gravy and hot coffee to feed a very sleepy army, and business didn't seem to slow down at all.

"Good thing you can't read your schedule." Holly slid

another tray of biscuit dough into the industrial oven. "I don't know what I'd do without you."

I wanted to point out that she'd said just a few hours ago that everyone in the family could survive without me, but my phone buzzed in my pocket. It was Teeny's school. This couldn't be good.

"Hey, Star, it's Sadie, down at the high school. Teeny's been caught fighting. It looks like she might be suspended, so you need to come down here and get her."

chapter
two

LESS THAN TEN MINUTES LATER, I arrived at Dead End High School. Sadie Kendall greeted me with a smile and a wave. She'd been the secretary when we'd been in school and didn't look much different except her hair had turned white. It lay in one heavy braid over her left shoulder, and she cradled the phone receiver on the other. She cupped a hand over the mouthpiece. "Have a seat, hon. I'll be with you in a minute."

I took a seat in one of the padded visitors' chairs against the wall of the small office. The morning had turned warm—not unusual for October in Central Texas—and I was glad for the air conditioning blasting from a vent above me. It reminded me of another day, in that same office, years ago when the campus housed K-12, instead of just the high school students. We shared one principal who was so distressed by what had transpired at school that day he drove me home himself. I tried to explain it wasn't my fault. It was Steffi Mae. She wouldn't stop talking to me during naptime and that's why I yelled at her. But he wouldn't even speak to me. He stared straight ahead as he drove me to the Mercantile. Granny explained later that Steffi Mae was a ghost, and not only that, but the principal's little sister, who had died years ago. That night Granny presented me with the amulet. It was just a simple locket. I could've sworn I saw Granny put something in it when I was peeking into the kitchen when the aunts were talking, but I never could open it. Granny placed it over my neck and told me when I wore it, I wouldn't see the spirits.

I lifted my hair off the back of my neck and the chain rose with it. When I tried to pull my hair free, the locket slid down the chain and escaped through the open clasp. Just then, a spirit appeared behind Sadie, and I tried not to make eye contact as I quickly retrieved the locket and stroked the cool metal. The spirit disappeared, and I shoved my amulet into my bra. It only needed to be next to skin to work, Granny had said.

I pulled out my phone, intending to kill some time with one of my puzzle apps, but found a voicemail from Granny. She wanted to know if I could come to work for a couple of hours. She said she'd get Tatty to run the register until I got there. If Teeny really was suspended, I would need to deal with that, but I doubted she would be. If she'd done something that serious, Grey would've called me himself. I texted Aunt Tatty that I would be there soon, hoping she got it, but knowing she wouldn't reply either way. We'd only recently gotten her to read the messages popping up on her iPad. It would be a whole other lifetime before we'd get her to text back.

I scrolled through my contacts and pulled up Zeke Fry, lifelong best friend of my cousin Boone, and manager of his bar. Pub Dead was next door to The Merc and while it wasn't open yet, Zeke lived upstairs above the bar, just like Granny and Aunt Tatty lived above The Merc.

He'd been there since he'd divorced Jessi-Lyn Gibson back when their daughter, Kira, was a baby. At least he'd gotten out of that relationship alive. My sister hadn't.

I'd no sooner sent the text to Zeke than the door of the office opened and Jessi-Lyn herself strode through. Every muscle in my body tensed. I still hadn't forgiven her for my sister's death and even in a town as small as Dead End, I could probably avoid her, except Kira and Teeny were best friends.

We stared at each other for a beat. Then Jessi-Lyn dismissed me with a flick of her eyes, as if I were nothing more than a part of the shabby décor of the front office.

"Hey Sadie, I'm here to get Kira." Jessi-Lyn hitched her large purse higher on her shoulder and glanced at her watch.

Sadie once again cupped her hand over the mouthpiece of the phone. "I'll let Principal Miller know you're both here now."

"Grey? I thought Kira was ill. You said I needed to come pick her up," Jessi-Lyn said.

"And if you hadn't hung up so quickly, you would've heard the rest of what I was trying to tell you."

"Which was?" Jessi-Lyn tapped her neatly manicured nails on the counter.

"Oh, yes, Mrs. Jenkins," Sadie spoke into the phone and turned her back to us. "I can send another form home with Lee. That won't be a problem…"

Jessi-Lyn turned back to me. "What does she mean, both? Why are you here?"

"Teeny was caught fighting, apparently." I shrugged.

"Who was she fighting with?" Jessi-Lyn asked. Then as my eyes widened as hers narrowed.

We both turned to Sadie, who nodded.

"The girls are out with Principal Miller now. I'm going to take y'all to them. Let me just get your visitor's badges printed out."

"I don't need an escort nor a visitor's badge, Sadie. I have my employee badge." Jessi-Lyn turned to the door. "Where are they?"

I knew we weren't getting out of there that easily. I had a suspicion Sadie enjoyed the power she wielded behind her desk—and possibly the drama unfolding before her. She'd been there so long everyone listened to her, even the Superintendent.

"You're employed at the middle school campus. Your badge doesn't work over here, so just hold your horses, and let me do my job, Jessi-Lyn."

They glared at each other for a moment, then Jessi-Lyn said, "Fine, then if I'm not considered an employee here, quit calling me by my first name and refer to me as Ms. Gibson as you would any other parent."

Sadie rolled her eyes. "Girl, I've known you since you were pooping your pants in the nursery down at First Baptist. You've always been Jessi-Lyn to me and always will be. Here's your visitor badge."

Jessi-Lyn and I both took our badges. Well, for Jessi-Lyn, it was more like "grabbed."

Sadie narrowed her eyes at Jessi-Lyn. "Don't make me call your Mamma and tell her how rude you're being."

To break up their staring contest I asked, "so where are we headed?"

"To the gym." Sadie stood up.

"Why?" Jessi-Lyn demanded.

"Because that's where Grey and the girls are."

"I'm not going to the gym." She handed her badge back to Sadie. "You can call Grey and tell him to bring the girls here. We can talk in his office."

I felt like I was missing something. What was so bad about the gym?

"The gym or here won't matter. Nessa is involved wherever y'all are."

Ah, there it was. There'd been rumors Jessi-Lyn and Vanessa Anderson, the high school girls' volleyball coach —and one of Teeny's favorite teachers—had recently broken up and that it hadn't been amicable.

"How is Nessa involved with my daughter? Kira quit volleyball, and she doesn't have her for any classes this year."

"I don't know. You'll have to ask her and Grey about that. Let's go."

Sadie knew. There wasn't much in this town she didn't.

The gym smelled the same as I remembered, and likely the same as all high school gyms across the country; stale sweat and basketball leather, with a hint of popcorn lingering from the concession stand that ran during events.

A couple dozen kids in matching putrid green gym uniforms were dribbling balls up and down the court, and the screech of shoes on the gym floor was as familiar as the smell had been.

"There's Grey." Sadie nodded toward the other end of the gym. "Both of my third period office aides are out, so I gotta get back."

He was standing in the doorway of the office the coaches shared. waved and motioned us over.

The last time I'd been in that office, I was fourteen and our gym teacher was giving me a warning about not dressing out once again. She'd asked if there was a problem with my health and if so, I needed a doctor's note because I was awfully close to failing P.E. But my reluctance to dress out had nothing to do with my health and everything to do with trying to avoid the ghosts on the basketball court. And no doctor would write me a note for that. And since Coach Williams refused to let me wear my amulet because it was considered jewelry, P.E. was more than the usual amount of miserable.

Teeny and Kira both sat on the bottom bench of the metal bleachers.

Grey was wearing his principal face. I'd only had a chance to see him in his official capacity once or twice. And it amused me. Grey Miller and I have been friends since his family moved here the day before Christmas break when we were in the sixth grade.

"What in the world is going on here? You two were fighting?" Jessi-Lyn asked.

Grey cleared his throat. "Today's fight happened in fourth period when they were painting signs for the pep rally and—"

"Kira was the one you were fighting with yesterday, too?" I asked. I shot Grey a look telegraphing my irritation that he hadn't told me that. We had agreed that Teeny wouldn't get any special treatment from Grey. She called him Grey when he came over to hang out, but on campus —and at all school functions—he was Mr. Miller. But dang, he could've given me a freaking heads-up instead of ambushing me.

"Yesterday? What happened yesterday?" Jessi-Lyn stood with her hands on her hips, staring down at her daughter.

"You didn't get the note about it?" Grey turned his gaze toward Kira. "I sent a note home, and it came back signed."

"Kira was at her dad's last night." Something in the way Jessi-Lyn's eyes narrowed at Kira for just a second told me that wasn't exactly true. And while Teeny had given me her note, it had been a generic one. Nothing indicating her fight was with her best friend since infancy.

Kira shrugged. "It was no big deal. Today isn't either."

"It was a big enough deal to pull me away from my students at the middle school." She turned back to Grey. "Since I didn't get the note, why don't you tell me what happened?"

"Coach Anderson broke up a shoving match between the two yesterday during lunch. She brought them to my office, and both of the girls claimed they were just horsing around. But in their "horsing around," one of them inadvertently elbowed another student in the face and gave him a black eye. And that's why they got detention."

"Believe me, Kodi doesn't need any help from us getting himself hurt. That kid slams his own hand in his locker at least once a week." Kira rolled her eyes.

Grey ignored her. "And then today, they were in the gym making signs for the pep rally, and apparently it began with throwing things—"

"Thing. Singular. Not things. I threw one thing at Teeny—"

"And how did all this happen, then? Your shoes are ruined. That's a hundred bucks down the drain," Jessi-Lyn argued.

"I never wanted these dumb shoes, anyway." Kira muttered. "Come to think of it, they look much better this way."

Jessi-Lyn made a face as if she'd found something in her refrigerator that had been there since last Christmas.

Teeny had remained silent during this exchange and continued to stare at her own reasonably priced department store sneakers, which were also covered in paint.

"You two are best friends. You don't go from texting for hours to covering each other in paint without a reason. What's going on here?" Jessi-Lyn demanded.

"Like you can talk," Kira muttered.

Jessi-Lyn stopped the pacing she'd been doing and didn't speak for a moment. Then slowly turned to her daughter and said with a clenched jaw, "This isn't about me and Nessa, Kira. We'll talk more about this tonight at home. Are we free to go, Grey?"

"Not yet. Coach Anderson wants a quick word." He glanced at his phone. "She's on her way."

"Nope. Not gonna happen." Jessi-Lyn turned to go and stopped in her tracks as Coach Nessa Anderson jogged through the doors of the gym.

chapter
three

"GOOD, you're still here. Before you all leave, Grey, can I talk to you in my office a moment?" Coach Anderson asked.

Grey followed her into the office that Coach Anderson and Coach Abbott shared—according to the engraved placard—and closed the door.

Jessi-Lyn fumed and ranted, threatening to leave anyway. But Kira spoke up. "Mamma, would you just stop? You're embarrassing me."

Just then, Grey motioned for us to join them in the office. The tension in the room was so thick it could've been scooped up and molded into a gaudy flea market ashtray.

"Coach Anderson has a few questions for the girls." Grey looked past me.

I hadn't seen him that uncomfortable since Carly and

I made him dress as Bowser to her Princess Peach and my Toad for Halloween several years back. That's when I realized he hadn't made eye contact with me the whole time. Which made him not telling me about the fight the day before even more suspicious.

Coach Anderson reached into her pocket and placed an item on her desk. I recognized the small black figure immediately. It was one of the voodoo dolls we sold at The Merc. She held the doll a moment before she spoke. "This is what Kira threw at Teeny."

"A cloth doll? Doesn't look like it could do much damage." Jessi-Lyn scoffed.

Coach Anderson let out a breath slowly. "It's a voodoo doll and I would like to know why they were fighting over it."

"Oh, for the love of... This is about us, isn't it? You're trying to get to me through my daughter. That's low, Nessa. Even for you," Jessi-Lyn said.

Coach Anderson opened her mouth, but Grey stepped forward and held up a hand. "Hold on now. Let's all take a deep breath."

"If my breath gets any deeper, Grey, I'm gonna hyperventilate." Jessi-Lyn never took her gaze off Coach Anderson.

"Coach, go ahead and tell them what you told me," Grey said.

"Yesterday in the hall after lunch, I found the girls

arguing. Then Teeny launched herself at Kira and looked like she was trying to take something from her.

"I blew my whistle, and they jumped apart, but Kira shoved something black into her jacket pocket. I asked them what they were fighting about, and they both said it was nothing. Because their scuffle hurt another student, I gave them detention. but I didn't pry into what their fight was about. Then today, I was supervising the Pep Squad for Mrs. Gerald because she went home sick. They were making signs for the Pep Rally, and I heard raised voices and looked over just in time to see Kira throw something at Teeny. It bounced off Teeny's face and slid under the bleachers. Teeny flicked a paintbrush full of paint at Kira and by the time I could get to them, they were rolling around in the paint. I sent them to clean themselves up, and I retrieved the doll." She nodded to the doll on the desk. "Turn it over."

I did as she said and something pink stuck out of the pocket that was sewn onto the doll. When we sold these at The Merc, we instructed the customer to write their wish on a piece of paper and tuck it into the pocket.

Jessi-Lyn reached for the doll, but Nessa pulled it out of her reach. She removed the paper herself and showed it to us. It was bulky and taped up as if it were a larger sheet of paper folded up. On the outside, written in red marker, were the letters N.A.

Jessi-Lyn said the words at the same time as I'd thought them. "Nessa Anderson."

Kira faced her mom. "No! That's not...we were only trying to..."

"Kira, don't!" Teeny spoke only two words, but I'd never heard such desperation in them. She didn't have a pigment of color left on her face.

Kira clamped her mouth shut.

"You were only trying to do what, Kira?" Jessi-Lyn asked. "Did Teeny talk you into doing magic? Did you try to put a curse on Nessa?"

"Mamma, this has nothing to do with anyone here. I don't know why we are even in trouble. It's our business." With the last part, she glared at Nessa.

Nessa shook her head. "You're not in trouble, Kira. At least not with me. I just wanna know about the voodoo doll. You can tell me."

"Y'all just stop the witch hunt for a minute," I said. "I don't know what's going on here, but even if this was some type of spell, why are you jumping to the conclusion that it is a harmful one? What if Kira just wanted the two of you back together?"

Jessi-Lyn turned to me. "There are no good spells, Star. I will not have my child involved with witchcraft."

Kira ignored her mother and faced Coach Anderson. "I swear, this is not about you. I don't know why the two of you had to break up, but it's not about that."

"Then what is it about Kira? If you don't tell me, you're grounded." Jessi-Lyn threatened.

Kira thrust out her chin. "I'm not telling you anything more. This is mine and Teeny's business and has nothing to do with anyone in this room."

With that, she crossed her arms over her chest as if she dared any of us to contradict her.

I thought Kira had called her mamma's bluff, but Jessi-Lyn wasn't done just yet. "Okay then. You are not to see Teeny anymore. I will not have you involved in this voodoo crap."

Teeny clamped her mouth shut—fury blazing in her eyes—then turned and ran from the room.

Kira followed but didn't quite make it to the door before Jessi-Lyn's hand shot out like a snake and grabbed her arm.

"Mamma! Let me go!" Kira tried to wrench free from Jessi-Lyn's grasp. "I need to go after Teeny."

"No, ma'am! You need to stay right here and explain yourself."

"You don't understand. As always, you don't care about anyone but yourself. Unlike you, I fight for the people I care about."

"And what's that supposed to mean?" Jessi-Lyn demanded.

"Maybe if you'd done the same, you wouldn't have driven Nessa away just when I got used to having her around."

Jessi-Lyn let go like she'd been bitten by a wildcat, and Kira darted out the door.

"Jess, I..." Nessa began.

Jessi-Lyn held up a hand to Nessa, then glared at me and said, "Grey, I want Kira moved out of any classes the girls share."

"Jessi-Lyn you can't do that," I stood and faced her.

"Oh, I can, and I have. Teeny is not allowed on my property. I will call the Sheriff if I see her anywhere near my house." She picked up her purse and strode out. I went after her.

"Jessi-Lyn, you're being ridiculous."

She ignored me and kept walking. I followed her from the gym out to the covered walkway leading to the main building. The bell rang and students started appearing like ants at a picnic. "Jessi-Lyn, stop and talk to me. Let's handle this like adults."

"Star, get out of my way."

"No, we need to talk."

We'd made it back to the main building and were having to weave our way through the throng of students. I reached out to grab her arm to stop her so I wouldn't lose her in the crowd. She had to see she was being unreasonable.

She tried to tug free from my grasp, but kneading biscuit dough several days a week gave me a stellar grip.

"Star. Let me go, or I swear to God I'll call the police and have you arrested for harassment."

The students around us stopped and backed up, encircling us. Some began chanting, "Fight! Fight!"

Jessi-Lyn used her teacher voice on them, "Get to your class or I'll report all of you to Mr. Miller. Don't think I don't remember your names either. I had every single one of you in eighth grade English last year!"

A tall lanky boy sauntered by and looked Jessi-Lyn up and down, then let out a low whistle. "Looking good Ms. Gibson."

She ignored him. "Let. Me. Go."

Just as she jerked away, I let go, and she landed on her ass in the middle of the ninth-grade hall.

I reached out a hand to help her up. "I'm sorry. Are you okay?"

"Get away from me," she hollered.

I took a step back. "Fine. You don't want my help. Got it. But you will not separate the girls. Teeny has done nothing wrong and I swear, you keep them apart and you'll regret it the rest of your life."

Jessi-Lyn scrambled up. "Are you threatening me?"

"Girl, if I was threatening you, you'd feel it. But you don't want to push your daughter away by curating her friends. It won't end well."

"You're telling me how to be a mother to my own daughter? You who have no relationship with your mother or any children? What right do you have to tell me how to raise a child? Astra is surely spinning in her grave at the job you've done with Teeny. She sneaks out of the house to come hang out at mine because she wants to get away from you. But now I guess she'll have to find some other place to go, because as much as I tried to be a mother to that child in memory of Astra, I will not have my own flesh and blood corrupted by the evil your family perpetuates."

I pointed a finger at her. "You're gonna lose everyone you've ever loved Jessi-Lyn Gibson. Everyone."

One kid nearby said, "Ohhhh...did she just hex Ms. Gibson?"

I'm not proud of this, but the fear in Jessi-Lyn's eyes egged me on and I said, "Damn straight!"

Jessi-Lyn turned and stalked through the crowd toward the front of the school. Good riddance!

The bell rang again, and the students slammed their lockers and scurried toward the open doors in the hallway. I turned to find Grey with his arms over his chest, giving me a look of disappointment.

chapter
four

I REALIZED Grey had been saying my name. I turned
and glared. "What!?"

"What the heck, Star? What kind of example are you
setting for the girls—or the rest of my students—fighting
with Jessi-Lyn after the girls just got in trouble for the
same?"

"You know she loves to push my buttons." Jessi-Lyn
had never been my favorite person, not when she was my
sister's best friend, nor when she'd been pulled out of the
lake and my sister hadn't.

"Just as much as you love to push hers." He glanced
around the now empty hall, and said, "Come with me."

"Are you going to give me detention?" I scoffed.

"I would if I thought it would do any good," he shot
back at me.

I followed him until we stopped at the music room

door. He poked his head in, and apparently finding it empty, ushered me in.

This whole thing had gotten out of control. I didn't like this side of Grey. Not one bit. "I need Grey for a minute instead of Principal Miller. Is that possible, or do I need to go home and wait for Karaoke tonight?"

Grey sighed, shook his head slowly, then said. "Fine. Hold on a second and I'll get him."

He wiped a hand in front of his face as if he were swiping a screen to change principal face into best friend face. The result was him cross-eyed with his tongue stuck out.

"You're such a dork." I gave him a small smile and some of the tension of the day melted away.

He pulled out a chair and sat, and I did the same.

"But as your friend, and not as Teeny's principal, I'm worried about her."

"Then why didn't you tell me about all this sooner? Why did I have to find out in front of Jessi-Lyn at the school?" Some of the tension crawled back into my neck.

He rubbed his eyes, then leaned forward in his chair. "I walk a fine line now that Teeny is one of my students, Star. My first duty is to her. I wouldn't have gone to any other parent yesterday and told them what it was Teeny's responsibility to tell you. She got detention, and you were notified about that and the reason for it. The details were up to Teeny to tell you if she wanted to. I have to respect that. As hard as it was. And today's events happened so quickly, I wasn't brought up to speed by Nessa on the voodoo doll until you were already at the school."

"I don't like it when you make so much sense." I gave him a small smile. "But Grey, you know Teeny. She wouldn't hurt anyone. The voodoo doll, whatever it is for, isn't for nefarious purposes."

"I know that, and I think Nessa does too. She just asked if she could speak to the girls about it and clear up any misunderstanding."

"But did you have to involve Jessi-Lyn? You know she hates magic and tries to pretend it doesn't exist. This brought back all sorts of crap for her."

He gave me a blank look.

"Astra's slumber party in the eighth grade?"

He shook his head slowly. "Oh, right, that's when Jessi-Lyn broke her nose. Does she still blame you for that?"

"Of course she does. When Zeke first started setting up playdates for the girls when they were little, she brought it up again and insisted that Kira wasn't to be left alone with me. It took years before she would trust me, and now, because of this stupid voodoo doll, she's banned the girls from seeing each other."

Grey crossed his arms over his chest and leaned back in his chair. "And did hexing Jessi-Lyn in the hall help that?"

"I didn't hex her. But her thinking I had made me feel

better in the moment." But not now. This wasn't about me. This was Teeny's life I was messing with. I gave him a quick squeeze. "I better go find Teeny. Talk later?"

"Yeah. Hey…uh…before you go, you talked to Carly lately?" He twisted the class ring he still wore on his ring finger.

"Not in a couple of days. She's been busy. I'll see her at karaoke tonight or rather we will. You're coming right?"

"I think it's just gonna be the two of you. I have some, uh…stuff to do."

"Y'all didn't get into another fight about the existence of aliens, did you?"

"What? No, we're good. I just think y'all need a girl's night."

"Yeah, we do! But you know you're one of the girls. If you change your mind, you know where we'll be." I leaned over and ruffled his hair. "See ya. Wouldn't wanna be ya."

I made my way to the front office to sign out Teeny and low and behold, Sadie was nowhere to be found. The poor woman's legs were being run off. Grey needed to get her some help. I removed my badge and placed it on her desk and signed the arrivals and departures clipboard. Kira's name wasn't on the sheet, so either Jessi-Lyn bypassed the office, or she was still somewhere in the building. I got the answer to that question as soon as I stepped out the front door. Jessi-Lyn and Nessa stood arguing a few feet from Jessi-Lyn's car, which was parked by the sidewalk. I glanced over and spotted Kira hunched down in the passenger's seat. I sighed. Maybe it was better I'd had an absent mother rather than one embarrassing me at school.

Aunt Tatty stood behind the register with a line of people a dozen deep waiting to pay for their purchases. She refused to use the tablet point-of-sale system I'd talked Granny into letting me install, and instead insisted on writing all purchases down by hand any time she was behind the register. This was the main reason we tried to make sure never to leave her alone in the store. Of course her sticky fingers might have played a small part as well.

"Let's go rescue Aunt Tatty," I said to Teeny.

She didn't answer but followed me to the register. We hadn't talked in the car. I didn't know what to say, and she didn't seem to want to say anything at all, so we'd mostly just listened to music. At least that was one thing we still had in common. She'd recently discovered Astra's old iPod touch in the attic and on it tons of songs that had been Astra's favorites, and Teeny was obsessed with them. I was fairly sure she was the only kid in her high school who knew all the words to *Kryptonite*.

"Bless your heart! You made it." Aunt Tatty stepped back from the cash wrap with her arms up like a good

Samaritan doing CPR when the paramedics show up. "Gayla had to leave to take one of her kids to the doctor."

I smiled and nodded at the customer at the front of the line and began wrapping her purchases.

"You have such a fun store. I wish we had one like this in our town," the customer said.

I returned her smile. "Thank you. It's been in our family since long before I was born. Where are y'all visiting from?"

One of her companions piped up. "Northwest Louisiana, up near Shreveport. We're here for a girls' trip. And to see if Dead End lives up to its reputation of being the most haunted town in Texas." She motioned to the two women standing in line behind her. They looked to be in their mid-twenties, and each had a basket overflowing with merchandise.

"We've been following Drusilla since her YouTube days." A blonde with pink tips held up Daisy's book.

"Is it true she used to work here?"

"It is. In fact, I'm her aunt." Aunt Tatty inserted herself into the conversation. Pride dripped from her voice, but it wasn't so much that she was proud of her niece, but instead pleased that she got attention for doing nothing other than being the aunt of a viral internet sensation.

I rolled my eyes.

"Really? You look so...*normal*." She gave Aunt Tatty a

once over, taking in everything from her sensible shoes to her eyeglasses hanging from a beaded chain around her neck.

Daisy was the millennial version of Elvira, without the big hair and plunging necklines. The persona she put on for the public and what she really looked like were night and day, literally. The death-obsessed goth girl with the jet-black hair and tattoos was a fresh-faced rosy cheeked strawberry blonde who was obsessed with sloths and chai lattes. Even her birth name screamed wholesome all-American girl. Daisy Lea Bell became Drusilla Von Leigh.

"Are y'all related to her too?" The customer nodded her head to me and Teeny.

"Yes, that's my other niece and my great niece," Aunt Tatty said, turning the attention back on herself.

The customer gave us scrutinizing looks as well. I was used to it. At least with the tourists. I suppose I did look rather plain if you held me up against Daisy and Mamma. None of the locals were that impressed with Daisy, since they'd known her before she was famous. Now Mamma? That was a different story. A Grammy winning country music star was more impressive than a self-proclaimed ghost hunter.

The first woman stood to the side with her shopping bag while I rang up the rest of the customers. "According to Dru, your store is one of the most haunted buildings in Dead End. Have you ever seen any of the ghosts yourself?"

A couple of the other women leaned in close for my answer.

Before I could speak, Aunt Tatty leaned forward and whispered, "I've seen ghosts that would make your toes curl. In fact, there are two in this store right now."

"Really?" The lady spun around. "Where?"

"Come with me and I'll show you. There's one on that ladder up there having a smoke, but the smoke is coming out through the hole in her chest." She pointed to the rolling ladder that was original to the store. Like one of those in a library. "And over there, by the tarot cards..."

"Why does she do that?" Teeny asked.

"What?"

"Lie to people."

"She doesn't see it as lying, I don't think. She loves to weave tales and I think she's just playing into the whole hoopla."

"And Daisy. She doesn't see ghosts either, but she's rich and famous because people think she does."

"True." That one was a sore spot with me too, but I tried not to influence Teeny's opinion of Daisy despite my own issues with her.

"So why haven't you capitalized on your own powers? You never even talk about your ability."

Ability. Curse. Bane of my existence.

"You keep your amulet on so that you don't...hey where is your amulet?"

I touched the bare spot between my collarbones and panicked for a second before I remembered it was in my bra. "The clasp broke."

"So why do you wear it? What's so bad about seeing ghosts?"

I couldn't tell her the truth, not all of it, so I told her part of it, "It just... It makes life...crowded. Does that make sense? Think about Dead End during October when all the tourists are here. Then double that number. That's what I see all the time. At least when I don't wear my amulet."

"Oh."

"When it first manifested, I couldn't be sure if I was seeing a real person or a spirit. It made for many embarrassing situations. And it gave me migraines."

"But now?"

"I've learned to navigate. Ghosts shimmer slightly too."

"Do you see them like...how they died like Aunt Tatty said?"

"No. They look alive. Just faded."

She nodded as if she was satisfied with that answer and we both sat there in silence with our own thoughts until Aunt Tatty's loud voice regaling a customer with more fake ghost news broke us from our reverie.

"What's her power?" Teeny asked. "Voice projection?"

I smiled. "You'd think, right? Aunt Tatty doesn't have any powers."

"Sure, she does. She can show up for work and manage to not really do anything while she's here. That's practically a superpower," Teeny said.

chapter
five

LATER THAT NIGHT, I opened the freezer to figure out what to cook for dinner. Aunt Mer had called when Teeny and I were on our way home and asked if I could feed Teeny before heading off to karaoke. She had to work late at the greenhouse. Which probably meant she was at Uncle Gavin's.

Usually that thought would make me smile, because I was rooting for the two of them, but tonight I needed her here. You're never too old to need your mom, in whatever form that relationship may take. Not only had Aunt Mer been more of a mother to Astra and me than Ruby Dee Bell had, she also never expected applause and fanfare for it. She had no clue about the day's events because I'd wanted to tell her in person. But I was sure if she did, she wouldn't want Teeny home alone tonight. I know I didn't.

I pulled up my contacts on my phone and clicked on Carly's name.

She answered with, "You better not be calling to cancel on me. I got here early and got us a table and I've sweet-talked Zeke into making us his brown butter nachos."

"Sorry, Car, Aunt Mer had to work late and I'm cooking dinner for Teeny." I pulled out frozen enchiladas and put them in the microwave to defrost.

"Okay, so you're gonna be a bit late. I can work with that. I'll flag down Zeke and tell him to hold off on the nachos."

"No, I..." I hated doing this, but Teeny came first. "I need to stay here with her. She had a rough day at school."

She was quiet for a beat, then said, "I understand."

Bless her heart, I knew she did. She was that kind of friend. But I could tell she was still disappointed. And we seemed to keep missing each other lately. With her crazy schedule as a deputy with the county Sheriff's department and my many jobs, we just didn't seem to be able to connect lately. "I'm sorry, Car. Why don't you call Grey? He said he had stuff to do, but maybe he'd drop it if he knew you were alone."

"You talked to Grey today?"

"Yeah, at the school. Teeny and Kira were fighting and—"

"You're kidding me."

"Yeah, it was a whole thing. That's why I'm staying home."

"Yeah, I get it. Wow, those two fighting would be like us fighting." There was something in her voice. I couldn't quite place it. She and Grey must have gotten into another argument like I'd thought.

"You don't have to stay home because of me!" Teeny appeared in the kitchen doorway. "I'm fourteen, not four. It's not like I'm not gonna burn the house down or eat candy for dinner."

"I'm not staying because I don't think you should be left unsupervised. I'm staying because I wanna be here for you. In case you need to talk."

"I don't. What I need is for everyone to quit thinking they know what's best for me and to freaking let me make my own choices. Quit with the helicopter parent crap! You're not my mother. You're not even my legal guardian. You're just my aunt, so back off and leave me alone." She stormed out of the kitchen and stomped up the stairs.

I slunk into the chair. Teeny's words hurt. But even worse, they were true. I was just her aunt. Nobody special. Hell, her own mother wouldn't even speak to me.

"That was rough. You okay?" Carly's voice drifted up from my phone on the table.

"Yeah. Sorry, I forgot you were still on the phone." I took a deep breath and made a decision. "I'll see you in twenty."

"I'll have a double margarita waiting for you."

I pulled the enchiladas out of the microwave, stuck them in the fridge and started to leave Teeny a note about how to finish defrosting and bake them. But if she could make her own choices, she could dang well figure out frozen food. And if not, well, cereal was always an option. So there. This helicopter was breaking formation.

Fifteen minutes later, I had a double margarita in hand and a promise from Zeke that our nachos were on the way.

"Is that Holly with Rowdy Kendall?" Carly squinted over my shoulder.

I turned and looked, then snorted. "Holy cow, it is! I guess she's run out of dates."

"Is she still doing her fifty dates challenge?"

I nodded and took a sip of margarita. Holly had decided that she wouldn't date anyone seriously until she had fifty dates with fifty different guys. "Yeah, I think she was somewhere in the high thirties the last I talked to her."

"I guess she could do worse. Rowdy seems to have calmed down since he came back to town and joined the force."

Just then Holly stood, grabbed her purse, and patted Rowdy on the shoulder, then headed our direction toward the door. I waved. "Hey Holls!"

She glanced over her shoulder, did a one-eighty, and slid into our booth. She nodded to my margarita. "I should've ordered several of those instead of the IPA I had."

"Bad date, huh?"

"Not bad, just mediocre. I thought if anyone, Rowdy Kendall would bring some excitement to the night. But he was distracted by something. Or rather, someone. He was texting constantly."

"Maybe he has a girlfriend?" I suggested.

"Could be," Holly said. "I saw the name Nessa pop up on his phone."

"Nessa Anderson?" I asked.

She shrugged. "Maybe? There was no last name, but it's not a common name."

"That's Teeny's Volleyball coach, Vanessa Anderson. Remember, she and Jessi-Lyn were dating for a while?"

She waved a hand in dismissal. "I know her by name only and I don't keep track of who dates who around here. But apparently Rowdy knows her well by the number of texts they were exchanging."

"Rowdy and Nessa aren't dating." Carly said.

Holly and I both turned to her. I raised my eyebrows.

Carly shrugged. "It's a small department. We talk."

"Well, whatever his wound, he seemed to be a decent guy otherwise. Well, except for being a cop." Holly winked at Carly and stood.

"Spoken like a true attorney," said Carly.

"Present company excluded, of course. You're one of the good ones." Holly blew Carly a kiss.

Zeke brought our nachos just as Holly sauntered off. He cocked his head, motioning me to scoot over, and bumped my shoulder with his. "What's this I hear about the girls fighting at school?"

I often wished I could go back in time and tell my teen-age self that Zeke Fry—#62 himself—would one day be hanging out with me like it was no big deal. It totally wasn't. My girlhood crush for him died the day he got married. No, earlier than that; the day he started dating Jessi-Lyn. And his divorce less than a year later didn't do a thing to resuscitate it. I shoulder bumped him back. "Yeah. Although I'm sure you heard a whole different version of the truth if you got your news from Jessi-Lyn."

"Nope, got it straight from Kira herself. Jessi-Lyn dumped her off earlier with a text that Kira got sent home from school and she couldn't deal with her right now and needed a night to compose herself," he said.

What a mother, I thought, but said, "How's Kira doing?"

"She's upstairs sobbing into her pillow. She asked to move in with me and says her Mamma has forbidden her to ever associate with Teeny or any of the Bell "witches" ever again.

Carly snorted. "Lord, Star, what did you do to Jessi-Lyn this time?"

"It's a long story, and I'd rather not go through it all again right now." I chugged the last of my margarita. "Let me get a few more of these in me first. And it's not the first time she's called me a witch. Remember Astra's slumber party in the eighth grade?"

"Who could forget that?" Carly shook her head. "I had nightmares for weeks."

"What'd you do? Turn someone into a frog?"

"Jessi-Lyn never told you about that night? Y'all were married for a year!"

"Come to think of it, she could jump really high, and I may have seen her eat a fly once. Or it coulda been a raisin." He grinned at me.

I narrowed my eyes at him. "You're lucky your brown butter nachos are near orgasmic, and that I can't actually turn people into frogs, because you might develop a sudden affinity for flies yourself."

He held his hands in front of him in a defensive position. "Hey, it's a legitimate question. I've seen stuff. I've been around your family more than other non-Bells—aside from Officer Do Good here—and I know y'all aren't a normal family."

"Is there such a thing as a normal family?" Carly asked. "My mother got religious and joined a cult after my dad died, and my brother, the original officer Do Good, is traveling the country with Drusilla Von Leigh, Mistress of the Dead."

I hid my face in my hair and shoved Carly's brother—he who shall not be named—far out of my mind. It was my fault he'd run off with my little sister. It was something that had almost driven a wedge between Carly and me.

"See, you proved my point. I know Daisy's thing is mostly an act. Hell, most reality tv is, but I saw her in action before she ever became famous. And don't get me started on your Granny. That lady scares me with the things she *knows*."

"And your best friend in the entire world? You think Boone's a wizard?" I asked.

"Oh, hell yeah. He's a wizard if there ever was one. You've tasted the beer here. And he does disappear a lot, leaving me to run things. He says he's off visiting his girl-friend, but I mean, we've never met her, so maybe he's on the council of wizards and he's handling council busi-ness." He grinned. "But go ahead, you Bell witches keep your secrets."

"We're not witches. We don't cast spells, we have talents. We don't have a coven; we have a family."

"If it quacks like a witch..." Zeke held his hands palm up and shrugged. "Enjoy your orgasm."

He was already back to the bar before I found the words. I turned to Carly. "What's that supposed to mean?"

"The nachos. You're the one who called them orgasmic."

"Oh." I shot Zeke an evil look, but he only winked, then turned to take care of a customer.

"You know we're not witches, right?" I asked.

Carly said, "I think the more important question is, why is that word so offensive to you?"

"Women accused of witchcraft were burned at the stake."

"Not in this century. Or the last, that I'm aware of. And you've seen Practical Magic. Witches are cool now. But if you want to be mad about it, blame your Granny. She's the one who advertises The Merc as being owned by descendants of Salem witches."

I rolled my eyes. I was gonna have a talk with Granny one day. Not that it would do anything but help me get things off my chest. The woman was as stubborn as a rock. "This is all Daisy's fault, you know."

"So, she's the one who gave you the gift of talking to the dead?" The corner of Carly's mouth slid up, and she raised an eyebrow at me.

"Gift? Ha! More like curse. But no, I mean all of this!" I waved my arm around. "The tourists that cause us to have to get here early to get a table at our favorite bar, the traffic, people calling us witches and thinking we're putting curses on them. If anyone but Grey was Teeny's principal, she probably would've been expelled today!"

"I know. I'm glad she wasn't, though." Carly pushed her plate away and sat back in her chair. "Hey, uh... speaking of Grey. I really need to get something off my chest before I explode."

"I've been wondering when you were going to bring it up. You two got into another argument, didn't you? What was it this time? Who the best Doctor is? I'm telling you; he will never change his mind about Eccleston."

"I—" Carly began.

"Star Bell and Carly Davidson are up next with *Tubthumping*, Zeke announced near the Karaoke station.

"It's our song!" I downed the rest of my drink and grabbed Carly's hand.

I was home by nine. Carly had the early shift in the morning. The house was quiet and there were dirty dishes in the sink, so I knew Teeny had at least eaten. Her door was closed, and her light was off. Either she was as tired as I was, or she was avoiding me. I scribbled a quick note and slipped it under her door. I couldn't stand us going to bed angry. So just in case she was still awake she'd know I loved her.

My last thought before I fell asleep was that Carly never told me about her and Grey's fight.

chapter
six

I SHOT STRAIGHT UP in bed and looked at the digital clock on my dresser. Just a hair after eleven pm. I'd been asleep for barely an hour, but it felt like half the night had passed. I was about to snuggle back down between the covers when my phone vibrated on my bedside table.

That's what had woken me. I scrambled to reach it.

"Star, can you come get me? And...bring...my extra inhaler." Teeny was breathing heavily.

"Where are you?" I leapt out of bed and was across the hall in the bathroom, digging through the medicine cabinet before she finished answering.

"On the corner of Pecan and Pine. Please come."

"On my way." I scrambled down the stairs and grabbed my purse and keys and slipped on shoes I wasn't even sure were mine. "Are you breathing through your nose?"

"Yeah."

She hadn't had an asthma attack in months. But it was terrifying for her—and me—every time it happened. I sped through the streets and kept her on the phone, reassuring her. And me.

When I pulled to the curb, she jerked open the door and slid in before I could even put it in park. I thrust the inhaler at her, and she took a puff. Once I knew she was okay, I headed home. Neither of us spoke until I pulled into the driveway.

"You not only snuck out of the house but also forgot your inhaler?" My hands shook. "What in the world were you thinking?"

"I wanted to talk to Kira. She wasn't answering my texts, and I had to talk to her, but when I got there, she wasn't home."

I realized then we'd been just a street over from their house.

"What was so important you had to talk to Kira tonight?"

"I don't want to talk about it. And you can't tell Aunt Mer!"

I turned off the car. I didn't like any of this. But Teeny didn't have to worry about me spilling the beans tonight; Aunt Mer's car was still gone.

"And I didn't forget my inhaler. I lost it." She stomped up the stairs.

As if that made it any better. But I didn't want to argue, so I just let her go. I crawled back into my bed and shut my eyes, but the comfortable sleep I'd had earlier wouldn't come.

Once again, I woke up disoriented, but this time when I sat up, sunlight streamed through my curtains. I reached for my phone, but it wasn't on my bedside table. I'd probably left it in the Jeep when I'd come back from getting Teeny. I put on my glasses, peered at my clock, and had just registered the shock of it being after eight when someone banged on the front door downstairs. That's what woke me up.

I peeked through the curtains and found two disturbing bits of information. Aunt Mer never made it home, and Carly's police cruiser was in my driveway. Oh God. Something had happened to Aunt Mer, and Carly was here to give me the bad news. I threw open my bedroom door, flew down the stairs, and sprang onto the wooden front porch, with, "Please tell me she's not dead!"

"Ms. Bell?" A tall stranger stood with Carly. And out in the yard, beside her cruiser sat a classic metallic blue Mustang.

"Yes? Who are you?" But as soon as I said it, I knew. I saw the badge he reached for, and who else but a fellow officer would Carly show up with on my porch this early.

"I'm Detective Palmer, with the Ingersoll County Sheriff's department. And I'm told you already know Deputy Davidson?" He nodded to Carly.

I gave Carly a closer look. She was slightly disheveled and her uniform rumpled. I'd last seen her less than ten hours ago, but she looked like she'd lived days in that time. In contrast, the Detective seemed to have stepped off the pages of GQ. Instead of a uniform, he was dressed in a tailored long-sleeve lavender dress shirt, and black slim fit dress pants. Both hugged his body like they were custom made for him. I glanced back at the car and despite its age, it was as shiny as this guy was. And sitting on the hood, was a strawberry blonde woman wearing cut-off shorts and a baseball cap. Most likely a ghost unless the dress code for law enforcement had greatly relaxed. I was careful not to meet her eyes.

The detective returned the badge he'd presented to me to its spot on his hip and took off his mirrored sunglasses. "Can we come in?"

I opened the door wider and let them pass. The wanna-be Daisy Duke stayed out by the Mustang. A cold front had come in the previous night and a chill swept in. It was then I realized I was wearing my Rug Rats pajama shorts and tank. Carly had gotten them for me on my last birthday as a joke, but honestly, they were my favorite pjs. I led them into the kitchen and sat in a chair at the table.

"Is Aunt Mer...did something happen?" Horrible thoughts raced through my head.

"This isn't about your aunt. We have some questions for your niece, Teeny." He said the name like it felt weird on his tongue.

"Teeny?"

He glanced at Carly. "That can't be her real name."

"It's real. It's not the name on her birth certificate—Christina—but nobody calls her that. What's this about?" My heart had only slowed down a bit. Had Jessi-Lyn called the police on Teeny for showing up at their house to get back at me? Not just the police, but this Detective Palmer. I looked him up and down. He was several inches taller than me, and his chocolate-brown eyes were framed by the longest lashes I'd even seen on a man.

"If you'd get *Christina*, I'll explain to both of you at the same time." He put emphasis on her given name.

"*Teeny* isn't here. She's at school by now." I crossed my arms over my chest. She may not have acted like it yesterday, but she was a responsible kid who always got herself up and on the school bus on time.

Palmer ran a hand over his closely cropped curls. "I was told she was suspended."

Panic gripped me for a moment, then footsteps sounded on the porch and the screen door opened. Relief filled me when Teeny appeared in the kitchen doorway.

"Uh, Star, why are the police here?" Teeny ran to me.

"Is Aunt Mer okay? She didn't come home last night. I got up early and her car wasn't here."

"Have you tried calling her?" Detective Palmer asked. "We didn't get any other accident reports overnight."

"Any other?" Teeny had picked up on that just as I had. "Why are you here?"

"I'm Detective Palmer, and I have a few questions for you." He pulled out a notebook. "Can you tell me where you were last night between the hours of eight pm and midnight?"

Before Teeny could open her mouth, I blurted. "She was here with me the whole night."

Carly shook her head sharply in warning behind him.

"Ma'am, I'm addressing Christina."

"What is this about, anyway?" I repeated Teeny's earlier question.

"I'll get to that, but first I'd like an answer to my question."

"And I gave you one. She was here with me."

"Star—" Carly began before Palmer interrupted her.

"Ms. Bell, why don't you go upstairs and get dressed so that I can question the child without interruption?"

"Child? I'm fourteen!" Teeny shot at him.

I crossed my arms over Chuckie and Tommy. I wasn't going anywhere.

"And if that's not possible, I might have to take her down to the station."

"You can't do that. You can't question her without me present. It's the law."

Palmer shook his head. "Texas law doesn't require a parent or guardian to be present during quest—"

"You're allowed to request a lawyer, though, and we can't question her until they get here," Carly said quickly.

Detective Palmer shot her a look that reminded me of a teacher I had in the third grade who didn't like us speaking up unless we were called upon, but to me, he said. "That is correct."

"Then that's what I want. I want to call my lawyer!" Except I didn't have a lawyer. Oh, but I did have a cousin who used to be one. I spotted my phone then on the counter, along with my keys. I touched the screen, but it didn't light up. "My phone's dead. It'll take a minute to charge."

"Use mine," Carly said. "Let me just unlock it.

I knew Carly's four digit unlock code; it spelled out her first dog's name—Yogi. She knew I knew it, but she took her time and when she handed it to me, her notes app was opened, and one short line of text stared back at me: *Be careful what you say.*

chapter
seven

"MY LAWYER IS on her way. Teeny and I are gonna go upstairs and get dressed." I grabbed Teeny's hand, and we exited the kitchen. My thoughts raced. What did Carly mean when she said to be careful about what I said? And what did this have to do with Teeny?

Teeny followed me into my bedroom, shut the door behind her, and slid against the back of it to the floor. "Why does that cop want to know where I was? I didn't do anything! Is he going to arrest me?"

"I don't know, honey. Holly is on the way; she'll figure this out." I didn't tell her what Carly had texted me. I didn't want her freaking out more than she already was. "Why weren't you home this morning? Where did you go?"

"I don't want to talk about it."

I closed my eyes and took a deep breath. "Teeny,

you're gonna have to. I need to know everything if I'm gonna be able to help you."

"It's not about any of this. I swear. I need to call Kira. Maybe she knows what's going on and she's still not answering my texts."

I let out a frustrated groan and jerked my closet door open. What I really wanted was to take a quick shower, or at least brush my teeth. I slipped a t-shirt over my head and wriggled into some jeans. I shoved my amulet into my bra and glanced out the window. The redhead was gone.

"It went straight to voicemail." Teeny plopped onto my unmade bed.

"Her Mamma probably took her phone away, honey. She was pretty pissed yesterday."

Tires crunched on gravel, and I peeked through the curtains and found Holly slamming her car door. She hadn't even removed her apron, which was covered in flour. The front door opened, and she hollered, "Star?"

I scurried to the top of the steps. "Up here!"

"Hold on now. Who are you and where are you going?" Palmer said from the kitchen.

"I'm Star's lawyer and I'm going upstairs to confer with my client."

"You're the lawyer?" Detective Palmer stood up. "Don't you own the biscuit place?"

"I do, but I've also passed the bar, Officer...?"

"*Detective* Palmer."

She held out her hand. "Detective Palmer, Holly Bell, Esquire."

He took her hand and shook it. "You really are a lawyer?"

"Not currently practicing, but fully licensed. And as I said, I would like to confer with my client before you question her."

"Sure." He waved a hand to the stairs.

I closed my bedroom door behind Holly, and she threw her arms around me. "What in the world is going on, Star?"

Teeny spoke up. "They want to know where I was last night."

"Oh. And where were you?" She knelt on the floor beside Teeny. "I need to know everything before the detective questions you."

"I snuck out last night and went to Kira's. She didn't answer the door, but she had something of mine I wanted back, so I climbed up the tree beside her bedroom and went in through her window and —

"You what? Are you nuts? You didn't tell me that part," I accused.

"I didn't want you to get mad."

"I'm not mad. I'm freaking furious. You could've died." Images flashed through my mind of Teeny's mangled and broken body lying at the bottom of a tree.

"I've done it dozens of times. I'm careful!" Teeny insisted.

"That's supposed to make it all better. So, you could've died dozens of times? And now, because of yesterday, Jessi-Lyn has called the cops on you. Typical vindictive b—"

"Ladies, focus." Carly put a hand on each of us. "So, you've climbed up that tree and into Kira's bedroom before? With Kira's knowledge and permission?"

"Yeah. Like I said, tons of times." She lowered her lashes.

"Did her mom know?" Holly asked. "Not about last night, I mean, but all the other times."

"Yeah, I mean the times she saw me do it, she said I should come through the front door like a normal person, instead of climbing up her hundred-year-old oak tree like a monkey. But she never told me I wasn't allowed to do it."

"Good. We can work with that. I don't think any of this will be a problem. You just answer the detective's questions honestly. But more importantly, don't volunteer anything he doesn't ask. Stop and think before each answer you give and make sure you're giving only the facts. If you need to, count to three in your head before you open your mouth. Give him as little information as you can give while still being cooperative. Does that make sense?"

I'd never had the pleasure—or rather legal difficulties

—of watching Holly in her role as a lawyer, but she seemed as sure in this as she was in anything and gave me total confidence.

"I think so," Teeny said.

"Well, let's go find out what's going on and handle it as it comes." Holly patted Teeny's arm and stood.

"Please state your full name for the record," Detective Palmer said.

"Teeny Bell."

"Is that the name on your birth certificate?" Detective Palmer eyed Teeny.

"Christina Elizabeth Bell."

"Where were you between the hours of seven and eleven pm?"

Teeny clamped her mouth shut—I could almost see her counting in her head—then said, "For part of that time I was here at home."

"And the other part?"

"I went to see a friend."

"And would that friend be Kira Fry?"

I didn't think Teeny could get any paler, but she did. "Yes."

Detective Palmer flipped through his notebook. "What time were you there?"

"I don't remember exactly."

I glanced at Holly, who gave me a reassuring smile. Teeny was doing so good.

"Do you think your friend Kira would remember?"

Teeny said, "No."

"Why not?"

"Because she wasn't home."

Detective Palmer placed the notebook on the table and leaned forward. "But you just told me you were hanging out with your friend.

"No, sir. I said I *went* to see her. But I didn't get to see her because she wasn't home."

Damn, she was good.

"Look, Teeny, I know you're nervous, but we can get out of here a lot quicker if you'd stop avoiding my answers and just tell me the truth."

"Are you calling her a liar?" I'd had enough of his attitude.

Holly put a hand on my arm.

"No ma'am, but she's obviously been coached on how to answer a question while not answering a question. And it's getting us nowhere fast."

"It would help if you could tell us why you're here, Detective Palmer," Holly said. "What crime has been committed and how exactly do you think my client is involved?"

"I'm investigating a suspicious death, and your client was seen at the scene of the crime last night."

"What?" Teeny jumped up from her chair. "Someone was murdered at Kira's house? Please tell me it's not Kira!"

"Kira is fine. She's with her father," Carly reassured her.

"Someone murdered her mother?" Teeny whispered.

"I didn't say anyone was murdered," Detective Palmer said. "But it's curious that's the conclusion you jumped to, Teeny. Why is that?"

"But you—"

"The deceased, Vanessa Anderson, was found at the bottom of the staircase. Cause of death is unknown."

"Coach Anderson?" The tears that had filled Teeny's eyes when she was worried about Kira now streamed down her cheeks. "Who would want to hurt her?"

"That's what I'm trying to figure out. And your name came up. A witness saw you crawling out of an upstairs window last night around ten pm. So why don't we walk through your night one step at a time?"

"I would never hurt her. I swear, I've never hurt anyone," Teeny vowed.

"What was your relationship with Ms. Anderson?" Detective Palmer asked.

"She's my volleyball coach."

"Did you get along? Did you like her?"

"Yeah. She is...was a good coach." Tears rolled down Teeny's cheeks.

"Did you ever have any problems with her? Ever get in trouble because of her?"

"No, I mean, kind of, but it was all a misunderstanding."

"What was the misunderstanding?"

"She thought me and Kira were trying to hex her or something with a voodoo doll. But we weren't...and her mom said we couldn't see each other anymore but I left something there and needed to get it back, so I crawled in through the window like I always do, and I swear...that's all I did. I was climbing out of the tree again when I..." She stopped the confession then and stared at the ceiling.

"When you what?" Detective Palmer prompted.

Teeny took a deep breath and looked me in the eye. "When I almost fell.

To my credit, I didn't even yell at her. We would have words later, but right now we had to remain a united front.

"When I got to the ground, I was out of breath and reached for my inhaler and it was gone. And my breathing got worse by the time I got to the street, so I called Star to come get me."

Detective Palmer raised his eyebrows at me. "*You* were at the house as well?"

"No, I met Teeny on the corner of Pecan and Pine."

"What time was this?"

"I don't know exactly. I can look in my call history to see what time she called me."

He nodded.

I grabbed my phone from the counter where it had been charging and found the time stamp. "She called at ten-oh-three, and we hung up when I got there at ten nineteen."

"Did you see any other cars on the street when you drove up?"

"I don't recall. I was concentrating on getting Teeny's extra inhaler to her in time, then when she got into the car, I was a bit busy making sure she was okay."

"So, this voodoo doll you mentioned earlier, is this it?" Palmer turned his phone around and showed us a photo. It was the voodoo doll with the initials NA, and it lay on the floor next to a pale hand.

chapter
eight

"I THINK I'm going to be sick." Teeny ran from the room.

"What the hell were you thinking, showing a photo of a dead body to a child?" I demanded.

"It was only a hand. And a woman is dead. I'm just trying to find out why. What is your relationship with Jessi-Lyn Gibson?" Palmer asked.

"Her daughter is my niece's best friend. We see each other socially. And I'm done answering your questions."

He glanced at his notebook. "Ms. Gibson also said you chased her across campus, pushed her down, and put a hex on her, in front of witnesses?"

"This interview is over." Holly stood. "If you want anything else out of my clients, you'll have to get an arrest warrant, Detective Palmer."

"I didn't hex her; I gave her some relationship advice." I blurted.

"I'll walk you both to the door." Holly turned and glared at me; a message that came through loud and clear. *Shut up!*

Palmer shut his notebook, and we got the standard, "don't leave town, be available for more questions" spiel, then thankfully they left. Carly barely even looked at me on the way out. For the second time in as many days, I felt blindsided by one of my best friends. Carly could've texted me to let me know they were on the way this morning.

After comforting Teeny, I sent her to the shower and came back to Holly, who was fixing breakfast. "You don't have to do that. You're not at work. Oh crap! Work! It's Friday morning, one of your busiest days."

"No worries. Deb and Sheri can handle it for a bit. Besides, you two need to eat and I don't imagine either of you is in any shape to manage the cooking yourself."

"We have cereal."

"Not even going to respond to that. You want to tell me about the doll?" Holly poured pancake batter onto a hot griddle.

I filled her in on the rest of what happened at the school and by the time I finished, breakfast was done.

"And Teeny never told you what they were really doing with the doll?" She placed the platter of pancakes in the center of the table.

"No, I didn't push her."

"You're going to have to before Detective Palmer questions her again. I need to know everything, so we're not blindsided again." She slid her chair back and stood. "I have to get back to the café, but we'll talk tonight," Holly said. "If y'all are still coming? I completely understand if y'all bow out under the circumstances.

"Tonight?"

"The float."

"Oh, right! The parade is tomorrow, isn't it? You don't think they'll cancel it? With a killer on the loose?" Dead Fest was a ten-day celebration leading up to Halloween in Dead End and the annual parade officially opened it. The family always got together the night before to decorate our parade float.

"No, I think if anything, the mayor will figure out a way to mention a murder just to help tourism." Holly rolled her eyes.

"Probably."

Holly hugged me and left.

I fixed a plate for Teeny and took it upstairs. I found her with freshly washed hair and clean clothes sitting on the edge of her bed with phone in hand.

"Holly made breakfast."

"I can smell." She didn't look up from her phone.

I placed the plate on top of her dresser. I'd checked my own phone while Holly was cooking. There'd been several missed texts from Aunt Mer. And a few from Carly. She *had* warned me they were on the way. I mentally retracted my earlier uncharitable thoughts.

I pointed to my phone. "Aunt Merilee is at work. She says she slept over there last night since she had a lot of work to do."

"Or Uncle Gavin to do," Teeny mumbled.

"So, you know about that too, huh?"

She shrugged. "Who doesn't? They're so obvious. Hey, did you tell her about all of this?"

"Not yet."

Teeny relaxed a bit. "Thanks. She'd rush home and ask me all the questions. I'm not ready for that. I just wish I could get in touch with Kira. Star, can you please take me to see her? Carly said she's with her dad. Can we go to the bar? I just want to see if she's okay."

I considered that for a moment. "On one condition, no wait, two conditions. First, you eat at least half of your breakfast, and second, I want to know where you were this morning."

She stood and grabbed the plate from the dresser but didn't speak until she'd eaten a forkful of pancakes and a bite of sausage. "I went to see my mom."

"Oh." I hadn't expected that. She never wanted to go to the graveyard when we visited. It was just up the hill from the house. I hadn't been there myself recently. I'd spent nights and days there shortly after Astra died, begging her to talk to me.

"I've been reading her diary. That's what I went to get that night at Kira's and I...I don't know what I wanted. I just felt like going to the graveyard, you know."

I nodded. "Did it help? Yelling at her?"

"How did you know I yelled?" Teeny asked with her mouth full.

"Because I did the same after she died. I was so mad at her for leaving me. For leaving you."

"Why did she leave? I mean, not when she died. Why did she leave Dead End and go live with Grandma Ruby?"

That was the million-dollar question. I stuck to the facts. "Grandma Ruby broke her leg, and Astra said she was going there to take care of her."

Teeny seemed to consider that. "And that's when she got pregnant with me?"

"Yeah, that's what Grandma Ruby told us when she brought you back to Dead End."

"And you didn't know anything about me until then."

I shook my head and smiled. "But I can barely remember my life before you came into it, kiddo." I reached my arms to her and for the briefest moment, she let me hold her.

"Her grave is a mess. Someone needs to clean it up." She wriggled out of my grasp and stared out the window toward the hill where the cemetery was located. "All the graves there are overgrown."

It was a small family graveyard on our property. No one in my family had died in my lifetime, so we hadn't had the opportunity to have a funeral there. But Granny insisted Astra have a headstone, so that we had some place to go and remember her. I had so many thoughts about that, but I stopped them there. I had a promise to keep to Teeny.

Pub Dead opened at eleven for the lunch crowd, so the doors were still locked. I peered through the glass and spotted Zeke and Kira sitting at the bar. She was crying, and he was rubbing her back. I was about to back away and tell Teeny we should come back in a bit when Kira spotted us. She jumped up and ran to the door. As soon as she got it open, she threw her arms around Teeny.

Despite the gravity of the situation, I couldn't help but feel a sense of relief. They'd made up from their fight and all was right in the world again. Kira was Teeny's person. Just like Carly was mine and when things aren't right with your person, nothing is right.

"So y'all heard what happened?" Zeke asked after the girls ran upstairs to his apartment.

I perched on one of the bar stools. "Yeah."

He ran a hand through his hair. "I just picked Kira up from school. They dismissed all the students for the day."

"Did she...see anything? This morning?"

"No, thankfully. She was with me last night."

"Does Jessi-Lyn have any idea what happened? She must be devastated."

"Not that she mentioned to me. She wasn't in a talkative state on the phone. Carly was trying to calm her down enough to get some answers from her, but she's shattered."

"Carly's been busy this morning."

When he gave me a quizzical look, I explained, "She and Detective Palmer from the county investigations unit came over and questioned Teeny and me at the house. Well, he did the questioning. She was just with him."

"What the hell? Why?" He put down the dishcloth he'd been wiping the counter with and leaned forward. "What would you or Teeny have to do with any of this?"

"Teeny snuck out last night to go see Kira and someone saw her climbing out the window. But it gets worse. You know the voodoo doll the girls were accused of hexing Coach Anderson with? It was found at the scene."

"You're kidding me?"

"I wish."

"Hey, there's your Aunt Merilee." Zeke nodded toward the window.

Aunt Mer marched past the bar toward The Merc.

"I wouldn't want to be on the other side of whoever's about to get an earful from her."

"Me either." I grinned. "This one time when Astra was eight, and I was twelve, we nearly burned the back field down and she yelled so much she ended up losing her voice for the rest of the day. After it was all over, Astra brought her a glass of water and told her, 'Next time maybe you should just write us a very angry letter, so you don't hurt your throat.'"

"Sounds like Astra. She was always so practical." His smile didn't reach his eyes. I was used to that when people talked about my dead sister. As if they weren't sure if they should bring her up. So, I deflected, as I always did, with sarcasm and humor so the other person knew it was okay.

"Well, one of us girls had to be."

"That was quick." Zeke nodded toward the window again.

Aunt Mer was back on the sidewalk and seemed to be looking for something. She dug her phone out of her pocket and a few moments later, my phone rang.

"Oh shit. You're her target," Zeke said at the exact same time Aunt Mer turned around and spotted me through the window.

I gave a little wave. What in the world had gotten her so riled up? I didn't have to wait to find out because she yanked open the door and barreled toward me.

AUNT MER DIDN'T YELL. It was worse. She cried.

Zeke wisely placed a napkin dispenser in front of her and then disappeared into the back.

"You didn't answer your phone. You didn't reply to any of my texts last night, or this morning. I was getting worried, and then I have to hear from Willa Jo that the police were at the house this morning?"

"I'm sorry you were scared. But Aunt Mer, I was worried about you too. You didn't come home last night and—"

"But I texted you and let you know where I was."

"My phone was dead. Then when I powered it up, I was dealing with a lot of other things."

"But you should have called or texted last night. I would have come home had I known Teeny had snuck out."

I wanted to tell her I was handling it on my own and she would have just made it worse, but although I was Teeny's godmother and closest living relative in Dead End, Aunt Mer was her legal guardian.

"And how in the world was she able to sneak out of the house, anyway? Nothing happens in that house that the rest of us don't hear."

"That's the truth," I mumbled.

"What was that?"

"Nothing. She didn't sneak out. She left when I was out with Carly, and I didn't know she was gone."

"You didn't check her room when you got home?"

"No, the light was off. I assumed she was asleep."

"What if she'd had an asthma attack, Star? You should always check on her before bed!"

She had, but I certainly wasn't going to bring that up right now. "I was respecting her privacy. She's a young woman now. She doesn't need us barging into her room all hours of the day and night."

Aunt Mer twisted the napkin in her hand. "Is it true she nearly fell out of the tree outside Kira's bedroom?"

"How in the world did you hear that?"

"Holly told Willa Jo and Willa Jo told me. When I heard, I came looking for you."

"So much for attorney client privilege," I said. But grateful Holly hadn't spilled the beans about Teeny's asthma attack.

"There are no secrets among the Bells, Star. You should know that by now."

"Really? *No* secrets?" Kira stood at the bottom of the stairs, with Teeny behind her. "Yeah, I'd disagree with that."

Aunt Mer ignored Kira's comment and rushed over to Teeny. "You okay, honey?"

"Yeah, I'm fine. What are you doing here?"

Aunt Mer turned back to me. "I'm taking Teeny back to the greenhouse with me. Where are you working today?"

"No, I don't want to go. I want to stay here with Kira," Teeny insisted.

"I'm not working anywhere. Teeny can stay with me and you can go back to work."

"No, I think I need to keep an eye on her. Teeny, get your things and let's go." Aunt Mer turned to me. "We'll talk more about this later. You've got to be more responsible, Star."

When the door closed behind them, I wanted to throw something, and I would guess Kira did too because she stomped back up the stairs. But instead, I took my energy out on the bar. It was almost opening time, and I'd kept Zeke busy with my drama, first by talking his ear off, then forcing him to the kitchen. The least I could do was help him get ready to open. I took the chairs off the table, propped open the front door, put the chalkboard sign out, and began rolling utensils into cloth napkins when I heard footsteps behind me. "It's safe to come out now," I said.

"You Bells don't scare me," Zeke replied.

"That's not what you said last night." I turned around and saw he had a plate of nachos in one hand and a drink in the other. "Zeke."

He shrugged. "You need to eat."

"I don't feel much like eating, but I can't let orgasmic nachos go to waste." I shoved a cheese laden chip into my mouth and smiled up at him.

He didn't return my smile. His gaze was fixed on something behind me.

"Hey Jess." He stepped out from behind the bar.

Jessi-Lyn stood at the door, more un-put-together than I'd ever seen her. Hair disheveled and wearing the same clothes she had on the day before. Her eyes locked on me, and she stormed toward me. "You! This is all your fault. You did this."

"I didn't do—"

"You hexed me. You said I'd lose everyone I loved and within hours, Nessa was dead."

She scrambled toward me like she was going to scratch my eyes out, but Zeke caught her in his arms. "Jess, come on, let's go sit down."

She shook him off. "No. I'm sorry. Star, please. You have to take off the hex. Please. I'll do anything."

"Jessi-Lyn, I swear, I didn't hex you. I wouldn't—"

"Come on, Jess." Zeke led her to a booth in the back.

I turned back to my nachos, but I had zero appetite. The lump in my throat wouldn't have let me swallow water at that moment. I scooped up my plate and took it to the back. When I came back out, a group stood at the front, waiting to be seated. I grabbed a stack of menus and went to greet them. Who needed a day off? Not me.

Teeny and Aunt Mer were sitting at the kitchen table when I got home that evening. Aunt Mer had cleaned up and Teeny looked a little less miserable. "How was the greenhouse?"

Teeny shrugged. "Same as always. Dirty. Green. Warm."

"What'd you do today? I figured you'd be here doing laundry since you had a day off," Aunt Mer asked.

"Doing laundry isn't my idea of a day off," Teeny said.

"Mine either. I ended up not having a day off, though. I hung out the rest of the day at Pub Dead and helped Zeke. A tour bus came in right after they opened, and I stayed to help and lost track of time." I didn't mention him being occupied with Jessi-Lyn.

Aunt Mer said, "How about pizza for dinner? We have to be at The Merc later to decorate the parade float, but what say we stop by Slicers and get your favorite, Teeny?"

"Is it okay if we don't go out? I don't really want to be in public right now."

"Okay, honey. I'll call Holly and tell her we can't make it tonight."

"No! I want to decorate the parade float. That's not really being in public. That's just being with family."

I wasn't sure how much of that had to do with the possibility of seeing Kira and how much had to do with her absolute love of the parade. The Bell family float was a yearly tradition.

"Sure, honey. Star, could you go pick up the pizza for us?" She turned back to Teeny. "We'll eat when she gets back, then maybe put on a movie until it's time to go?"

I really wanted a shower and a nap, but I nodded.

Slicers was packed, and people waited outside to be seated. The hostess directed me to the bar to pick up my to go order. I spotted the only empty bar stool and went to wait for our pizza. I spotted Grey a few bar stools away and threw an arm around him. "Hey you!"

"Hey! What are you doing here?"

"Picking up a pizza. I heard about Coach Anderson. How are you doing?"

"Peachy keen, Dimples."

He hadn't called me "Dimples" in a couple of decades.

"About to head to the football game. Can't cancel football just because one of my teachers is dead, can we? Superintendent says distraction is what we all need. Screw that. What *he* needs is a championship." He thumped the empty beer mug down on the bar a bit too forcefully.

His eyes weren't only glassy because of tears, he was drunk. I knew Drunk Grey. This wasn't good. Drunk Grey got us both kicked out of the prom our senior year and was going to get himself fired if he didn't chill. I wasn't going to let him ruin his career. "Let's get you home."

"Home? I can't go home. We have a game to win. I mean, that's all that's important, right? Stupid football!"

A couple near us sporting Dead End Spirits jerseys turned toward us. I turned too, as if I had also heard what they heard and was trying to figure out where it came from. I shrugged.

I leaned in close to Grey, close as a lover, whispering sweet nothings in his ear. Except there was nothing loving in my voice. "Listen to me. You stand up, try not to wobble, and follow me to my car now. If you don't, I'm going to announce to the entire bar what your middle name is. Got it?"

"You do that, and I'll tell everyone about prom night," he whispered back.

He was staring into his beer so he didn't see the look

of horror that had surely passed over my face, but just as quickly he said, "No, of course I would never do that. I'll take it to my grave. But yeah, I'll go with you. I need to pay first."

He signaled the bartender and after Grey took care of his business, I said, "I'm here to pick up a pizza, under the name Merilee Bell, but is there any way I can change that to delivery?"

"Sure, but it's ready now. I can just send it with you."

My stomach rumbled, and I wished I could do just that. "I'm not going to make it home just yet, and there are hungry people there waiting for it. I'll pay extra for delivery, along with a generous tip."

The guy nodded, and I left the cash, then led Grey to my Jeep. After I buckled him in, I texted Aunt Mer. *Pizza's on its way, I'll meet y'all at The Merc. Have to take care of something first.*

I wasn't at all sure how I was going to do that.

chapter
ten

GREY LIVED IN HIS PARENTS' house. Which had also been his grandparents' house before them. It reminded me of Norman Bates' house, except it was on a family friendly tree-lined street instead of on a hill at the edge of town. And his mother wasn't a creepy skeleton in a rocker. She and his dad were both very much alive and traveling around full time in an RV across the country.

"One step at a time, buddy," I said.

"But look how long my legs are. I could take them all at once."

He wasn't wrong. He was at least half a foot taller than me, and I was already on the tall side. "But that's probably not a good idea, is it? Where are your keys?"

"Keys? We don't need keys where we're going!" he said in an exaggerated accent.

"Okay Doc Brown, where we are going is into your

house, and yeah, we definitely need a key for that. Unless you plan to break a window. So, you got a set of keys in those pockets somewhere?"

"Oh, breaking a window would be fun. Let's smash them all out. I hate this dump." He leapt off the porch. "I'll go find a big rock. I keep tripping over one by the tree there."

"No! Holy crap, Grey. Come back here." I hadn't seen him like this since graduation night. I chased after him. "You cannot break your window."

"I'll do whatever I want." He slurred his words, and it came out *wheveriwant.*

"Are your keys in your pocket?" I moved toward him, but he dashed out of my reach.

That was it. I'd had enough. I ran and tackled him to the ground. He landed face first with me on his back. I was afraid for a moment I'd knocked him out. Oh hell, what if he'd hit his head on the rock he was searching for? I scrambled off him and peered into his face. "Grey! Are you okay?"

"Yeah, but what the hell, woman?"

I stood up and held out my hand. "Get up and come inside."

He rolled over. "You're so mean. I should give you detention."

"I'm already there. Now give me your damn keys."

· · ·

I managed to get the door unlocked and get him into the house and onto the couch. That's as far as I planned on going. No way was I going to try to get him up the narrow, creaky stairs to his bedroom. I made my way to the kitchen, poured him a glass of water, and brought it to him.

He was sound asleep. I knew I should probably wake him up and make him drink water so he wouldn't be so hung over the next day, but maybe the hangover would teach him a lesson. I wasn't completely heartless, though. I took off his shoes, then went back to the kitchen, found aspirin, paper towels, and a container to serve as a puke bucket and placed them all on the coffee table by the sofa. I went upstairs then and grabbed his pillow and a blanket and took it back down.

Just then, the front door floor open and Carly stepped through the door. She stopped when she saw me, and her shoulders relaxed.

"Hey, what are you doing here?"

"I got a call to this address for a domestic disturbance. What's going on here?" Her voice caught some place between cop and best friend.

"Simmer down, Deputy Davidson, it's all good." I smiled and filled her in on the night's events, finishing with, "some nosy neighbor probably saw me tackle him and thought we were having a lovers' spat."

"You tackled him? For real? I hope the neighbor got

that on video. I would pay top dollar for that footage."
She smirked and ruffled Grey's hair.

Grey's eyes fluttered open, and he stretched out a
hand. "You're here. I'm so sorry about earlier."

Carly looked at me, then at Grey. I grinned. We'd both
experienced sleepy Grey before. He'd fallen asleep so many
times during study sessions and was like a cuddly baby. We
found if we just played along with whatever he was asking
—like the time he asked if the moon was still naked—he'd
fall back asleep. But Carly didn't smile back. I was about
to grasp Grey's hand and reassure him, but Carly lowered
herself to the floor and placed her hand in his.

"Me too. You sleep now and we can talk about it
later."

He nodded and kissed her hand. It wasn't the kiss of
two friends making up after an argument. And neither
was the way Carly stroked his cheek.

"How long?" I asked. I felt like I had swallowed a
bowling ball.

"A bit over a month. He wanted to tell you, but I
asked him to let me. And I tried, Star. That night at
karaoke."

It all made sense. Him pushing us to go on a girl's
night out. She insisting I come out when I knew I should
have stayed home with Teeny. I shrugged and stood.
"What's to tell? My best friends are dating each other. I
mean it's not like either of you owe me an explanation.

But a month? You waited a whole freaking month to tell me? We don't keep things from each other, Carly. At least I thought we didn't."

"But you've been keeping stuff from me too."

"Like what?"

"Like freaking everything! You said Teeny got sent home from school for fighting. You said nothing about the voodoo doll and the objects that were in it."

Grey rolled over and reached for Carly again. She disentangled herself from him and said, "Let's talk on the porch."

"Will I be talking to my best friend, Grey's girlfriend, or Deputy Davidson?"

"Your best friend. Everything is off the record. But please tell me everything so I can figure out how to help you. It's not looking great for Teeny."

We sat in the swing, and I told her about everything that transpired in Grey's office and finished with, "but I'm sure you already heard all this from Grey."

She was quiet for a moment, then said, "Actually, he didn't. Which is part of the reason we fought earlier."

"You two got into a fight?"

"Yeah, that's why he was drunk at the pizza place. Because I questioned him about what Jessi-Lyn had told us. Not as his girlfriend, but in an official capacity."

"It's so weird to hear that word from you."

She shoulder-bumped me. "I know. It's still a bit

weird for me. Anyway, he told me if I wanted information about his teachers and students, I'd have to get a warrant."

"Ouch. But I mean, I can see his point."

"It's not like I like being in the middle of this."

"How'd you get assigned to this case?" I asked. "You don't normally work with the detectives."

"I was the first officer on the scene. Detective Palmer came later, then Sheriff Briggs assigned me as his assistant on the case. But I'm not sure how long I'll get to stay on the case. Palmer dressed me down this morning after we left your house." She laid her head on my shoulder, and we sat in silence for a bit.

"Does Palmer really think it's murder? And what was Nessa doing in the house, anyway? She and Jessi-Lyn were broken up."

Carly sat up straight. "I can't talk about the case, Star."

"You just sat here while I told you everything I knew, and you can't share anything?"

"I want to. You don't know how badly I want to, Star. I know neither you nor Teeny had anything to do with this."

"But?"

She sighed. "I get it now. Just like Grey was doing his job earlier, I have to do mine. Star, you just make sure you do yours."

"Which one would that be? Serving drinks, serving

breakfast, or playing referee between Granny and Aunt Tatty?"

"Protecting Teeny. Merilee might be her guardian, but you're her protector. Your Mamma knew exactly what she was doing when she brought Teeny to you. You fight for those you love."

chapter
eleven

I PULLED onto Main Street and parked in front of The Merc. I was the last to arrive, if the various family vehicles littering the street were any indication. I let myself in through the front, so I had time to center myself before facing the mob. I adore my relatives—most of them—but as with any large family, when you get them all together, they are a lot.

"Star, honey, is that you?" A voice called from the top of the stairs.

"Granny? What are you doing up there instead of out back?"

"I was waiting for you. Now get your booty up here and talk to me."

"Coming!"

Granny sat at her table, shuffling her cards. "Close that door, will ya, honey?"

The door in question led to a common area shared by the two upstairs apartments where Granny lived with her sister, my great-aunt, Tatty. Tatty and Granny had lived together as long as I'd been alive and sometimes it seemed like they'd be here long after I died.

I did as she said and took a seat across from her. "Why were you waiting for me? Why didn't you wait downstairs where there's food? Have you eaten?"

"Hey, I'm the grandma, that's the question I'm supposed to be asking and by the looks of you, you aren't eating nearly enough."

My stomach growled in response. "Believe me, I eat plenty. I just haven't eaten today since..." When? Breakfast?

She made a noise in her throat that meant something close to *I told you so* and reached around to one of the chairs, grabbed a foil covered plate, and handed it to me. "Eat."

"I'm not eating your dinner, Granny. I can go downstairs and get something after we're done visiting."

"That's not my dinner. That's yours. I already had mine. See." She pointed to her blouse, where I spotted a few crumbs as she dusted them off. "I had Merilee save you a plate in case Willa Jo's bunch ate everything. So, you eat, I'll read your cards, then we'll talk."

There's no arguing with a grandmother who wants to feed you, so I dug into the feast comprised of Holly's garlic cheese biscuits, Aunt Mer's cookies, Aunt Willa Jo's chopped brisket sliders, and various other family favorite dishes. And found I was hungrier than I'd thought.

"How are you, honey?"

"Much better with this." I took a big bite of Aunt Mer's peanut butter cookie.

Granny's ability was reading people. She didn't read minds, but rather emotions. She cocked a penciled-in eyebrow at me. At the age of ninety-eight she was still quite vain. She didn't wear a ton of makeup but penciled in her eyebrows every morning and I swear I've never seen the woman without lipstick. Not even when she was in the hospital a few years ago.

She laid the cards in front of me and said, "Turn them over one at a time until you come to a major arcana card. Then turn over the next two cards immediately after."

I did as she said and revealed The Lovers, Five of Swords, and Ten of Cups.

Granny snorted. "Just as I suspected. You're not *fine*. Why in the world would you lie to an old woman? I could die any minute and your last words to me would be false."

"Granny, I think you're gonna outlive us all. But I wasn't lying to you. I'm not great, nor am I in the depths of despair, so I'm fine." I flashed my dimples at her. "Besides, you're reaching. The Lovers is a good card."

"It can be, but that's not what I'm seeing. You found

your soulmate, but someone else has their heart. Someone you care a lot about."

I sighed. "Granny, I've asked you not to speak his name in front of me."

"I wasn't talking about R—"

"Shhhhh!" I waved my arms.

"For Pete's sake, child, you are the second most stubborn woman I know."

"And who is the first one? You?"

"You better believe it! All I'm trying to tell you is this one—The Ten of Cups—says you're going to have a happy ending after all."

"Yeah, not gonna happen. Believe me. That ship has sailed, sunk and is buried at the bottom of the ocean, never to be found again, not even if James Cameron wanted to."

"James who?"

"Never mind Granny, I was just being a smartass."

"Better than a dumb one." She picked up the deck of cards, leaving the three out there. Then spread them in front of me. "Pick one more. We need a clarification card."

"I really don't want—"

"Do it."

"Fine." I revealed the Eight of Pentacles. "See, it's reversed. Reversed cards are bad. You can't argue with your own cards. So there."

She gave me a look that was just this side of condescending, but also a bit excited. It was the look she wore when she was about to teach me something new about tarot cards. "Gosh no, honey. There are no bad cards. The cards only help you see what's already there. They don't cause anything to happen. The Death card, for instance. People are always thinking they're gonna drop dead when it comes up. It's not about literal death at all, but about change. Reversed cards are just another way of interpreting the message. A lot of times, a reversal will point to the inner self instead of the outside world. For instance, The Eight of Pentacles upright usually points to skill work. Perfecting your craft, whatever that may be. But reversed, it's about working on yourself."

"What does that mean in connection with the other cards?"

"I think it means that to get your happy ending, you need to focus on your own happiness. Figure out what you want in your own life."

"You've been talking to Holly, haven't you? She's been trying to get me to quit some of my jobs."

"Honey, you chose the cards. I'm just telling you what I see. And no, I've not talked to Holly—at least not about you—but if you need to quit, I won't be upset."

"I don't want to quit, but you really need to let us hire help soon. The crowds are getting bigger and bigger each year, and Aunt Tatty refuses to help with the register."

"Not sure if I want her at the register, anyway. But

don't you worry, the right person is coming, dear. I won't hire just anyone, you know."

"But I don't think anyone is going to come in and ask for a job unless you put a help wanted sign out."

"Don't be so sure, dear." She gathered the cards and began shuffling them again. "Do you see anything new in my parlor?"

Granny's *parlor* doubled as her sitting room and her office, but the décor leaned toward the macabre and mystical since that's what her clients expected from her. Her chair was an ornately carved wingback covered in plush, dark purple velvet which contrasted nicely with her snow-white hair. The walls were also dark and filled with various paintings and portraits of our ancestors. She didn't have a crystal ball, but she had a scrying bowl and several decks of tarot cards. And a candelabra sat on the mantle. Aunt Mer was always trying to give her those battery-operated candles because she was afraid Granny was going to burn down the place, but Granny had told her she'd lived with candles safely for longer than Aunt Mer had been alive.

I continued my survey of Granny's parlor and finally spotted something new. A framed magazine article on Granny's wall. It was from an issue of *Haunted Heartland* magazine from a few months ago. There was a box they'd highlighted with a quote from granny that said, "The Bells are descended from Salem witches." Along with it was a photocopy of a painting of our purported ancestor. Despite the size and graininess and I could definitely see the family resemblance to Granny. But everyone knew the Salem "witches" weren't witches at all, but rather everyday women the patriarchy tried to get rid of by accusing them of awful things.

"You like it?" Granny nodded at it. I had Willa Jo cut it out and frame it for me so the customers could see it.

"If you like it, that's all that matters. It's your parlor, after all."

"That's not an answer. What's up, honey?"

I told her about Jessi-Lyn and the subsequent conversation Zeke and I had about witches at Pub Dead that night. "And you don't do anything to dissuade that belief."

"Because we *are* witches, my beautiful girl."

"I wouldn't doubt you are, but I'm not."

"How would you describe a witch?"

"Someone who casts spells and does magic. But I don't do either."

"Don't you? Do you make a wish when you blow out your birthday candles?"

"Yeah, but—"

"Do you ever wish upon a star or throw salt over your shoulder? Witches don't wear pointy hats and ride brooms. Witches are powerful women who change the world with their words."

"I am definitely not a witch in that case. I haven't done anything noteworthy my whole life."

"Girl, you're changing the world just by being in it. And your life isn't over yet, my dear. Tell Zeke to come see me sometime. I don't see the boy often enough."

I was reeling from the whiplash caused by the abrupt change of conversation when Granny pulled a small tool set from her apron pocket and said, "Now let me fix your amulet."

"How did you know?"

"A witch always knows." She tapped her index finger to her nose and her laughter filled the room. "Silly girl! Because I can put two and two together. It's not around your neck, and there is a small bulge in your bra. And if that's not your amulet, you need to see a doctor."

I reached into my shirt and pulled out the locket and chain. I dumped both on the table and focused my gaze on the lace tablecloth.

"You know, everyone has to take the training wheels off sometime."

"What's that supposed to mean?" I asked.

"You know exactly what I mean. I made this for you when you were a child. When you needed it—"

"I still need it. You don't know what it's like. They're everywhere." I jerked my head up to prove my point, quickly glancing around the room, trying not to make eye contact. "There are two spirits in here, possibly a third one, but that one is really faded."

"Faded?"

"Some are as solid as you and me, but some look more like a hazy hologram." I shut my eyes again. "Like Astra was in the beginning before..."

"Maggie mentioned that once."

Granny never spoke of my Aunt Magnolia. She was the only other one in our family who could see spirits, but she disappeared years ago. I waited for Granny to finish, but instead she handed me the locket.

As soon as my skin touched it, all the spirits disappeared, and I let out a breath I was very much aware I'd been holding in.

"My point is the spirits don't control you. You are alive. They aren't. If you took off your training wheels and tried—"

"Thank you for fixing my amulet, Granny." I fastened it around my neck and took the locket between my fingers, rubbing it reassuringly. "I'm happy with my life the way it is."

Granny snorted. "Lie to someone who might believe you."

"What are you lying about?" Aunt Tatty asked from the doorway.

"None of your business, Tatty. I'm trying to have a private conversation." Granny asked her. At the ages of ninety-eight and ninety-three, they still bickered as if they were teens having to share a room.

"I came up to get my sweater if you must know, unless you *borrowed* it again, Adelaide. Hey, Star!"

"Hey, Aunt Tat." I gave her a wave.

"Since Star's here now, why don't you get her to help you downstairs so you can join the party?" Aunt Tatty said.

Granny rarely left her apartment these days. We'd tried to get her to let us put in one of those chair lifts on the staircase to help her down, but she said the store hadn't changed much in the years since she owned it, she would not mar it now to put in some old lady device when she wouldn't need it for much longer. Boone threatened once to throw her over his back and carry her down piggy-back style. She'd dared him to try.

"No, I think I'll go lie down. I'm feeling a bit tired." She put the cards down and stood up, balancing her weight on the handle of her cane.

"If you change your mind, holler out your window and I'll come back up and get you." I smiled and leaned down to give her a kiss.

She grabbed my hand and whispered, "Take off those training wheels and you might find out what happened to the coach."

chapter
twelve

GRANNY'S WORDS rang in my ears all the way downstairs and I didn't hear a word Aunt Tatty was saying to me. I followed her out to the back alley. What could a spirit tell me that would help anything?

"What in the world happened to you?" Aunt Mer stood in front of me with her hands on her hips.

I explained about finding Grey drunk at the pizza place.

"I wish you would have called instead of sending that cryptic text. Teeny was worried out of her mind. The girl is completely frazzled." She nodded toward the float where Teeny sat.

She looked calm enough to me. And if she was frazzled, it was because of the tissue paper flowers she was making. She and I both hated those flowers. Our family had done the same thing for years because we couldn't figure out much more to do. Yet another sad commentary on my life in general.

I would love to do something with lights or glow sticks, but that wouldn't work, since the parade was a morning event. Which was also dumb. I'd long been a proponent of moving the parade to nighttime, because a daytime Halloween parade was like having a Christmas parade in January. This was yet another reason Aunt Willa Jo needed to win the election.

"Kira's not here?" I scanned the many faces in the alley, surprised that Aunt Magnolia's husband—and Boone's father—Uncle Buddy was making a rare appearance. Isaac was there cleaning off the faces of his young siblings, Aunt Willa Jo's late in life *oops babies*, Fox and Mal. Zeke was also present and currently perched on a ladder, attaching chicken wire to a frame. He wasn't biologically related to us but was usually at most family gatherings since he and Boone had been best friends for decades.

"No, I think Zeke said she's with Jessi-Lyn, but is supposed to be coming later."

"You okay, hon?" Aunt Willa Jo, the youngest of my aunts, stood in front of me. At the age of fifty-four, she dresses and acts closer to my age, and she has the body to carry off the look and even if she didn't, her attitude would do it for her. That day's outfit was black yoga pants with a hot pink t-shirt that said, "Namaste in Bed." A tied died scrunchie held her mahogany brown hair in a messy bun. "Holly told me all about that jerk detective grilling you and Teeny."

"Yeah, I'm fine." I gave her a hug as you do in southern families, even when you've seen that relative just a couple of days ago. She smelled of patchouli and orange. "With everything that's going on, honey, I don't want you to worry about putting out campaign signs for me. I can get someone else to do it. You're working much too hard, and now with this whole thing, you have your hands full."

"No, I want to do it. Really, I do. It'll give me something else to think about, plus it will get me outside."

"They don't have to go out for a few days, so if you change your mind, don't give it a second thought."

I promised her I would, and she and Aunt Mer went on about their business, but I couldn't quit thinking about what Granny said about talking to the ghosts about things. It made sense. Ghosts saw everything, which is why there were wards on our house to prevent them from being inside. But it wasn't true for The Merc, at least not the public part of it. I slipped away from the parade prep.

I was just about to pull the amulet over my head when a tap on the front window nearly made me jump out of my skin. Kira stood there waving her arms at me. I dug my keys out of my pocket and unlocked the door to let her in. She was as pale as the moon overhead.

"Hey there! I thought you were with your mom."

"She just dropped me off, but...she's pretty upset. I don't know what to do. Can you go talk to her?" She motioned to the row of cars outside.

I spotted one of them with the headlights on low idling in a space a few spots from the entrance.

"Me? Why don't I go grab your dad? He's out back."

"No, she specifically asked me to get you."

"Really?" I guess she wasn't done taking her grief out on me. In any other situation, I would've said no, but Kira looked desperate. "Okay, honey. Teeny's out back and there's food. You go on out."

She all but ran through the store to the back.

I locked the door behind me and approached the car with the headlights on. Jessi-Lyn rolled down the window. "Can you get in?"

"What's going on?"

Instead of the sarcastic retort I usually got from her, she only said, "Please. I just want to talk to you."

As soon as I closed the car door, she said, "You have to un-hex me."

"Jessi-Lyn, I told you before, I didn't hex you."

"It's okay, I get it. I know you were always jealous of

mine and Astra's friendship, and you still blame me for her death...and the things I said about Teeny, I didn't mean them. And Astra would be proud of the way you're raising her. She's a good kid. I've told Kira she can hang out with Teeny again. I brought her here." She motioned to the store. "See, I'm making an effort, so can you please remove the curse?"

So that's what was going on. She was terrified and thought I could fix it. If only I could.

"I'll do anything." She grasped my arm. "I just don't want to lose anyone else."

"I don't want you to lose anyone else either, but I didn't do anything. I swear."

She ignored me. "My Mamma called today. She went in for a routine mammogram and they saw something on it and now they want to do an ultrasound. Please, I'll do anything. Remove the hex. I can't lose my Mamma too."

I sighed. My heart hurt for her. "You're giving me too much credit. I wasn't hexing you. I was just trying to make you see how you pushed people away. I didn't cause Nessa's death. I can pray for your Mamma, and I will, but I can't change her fate. I don't control life and death."

She let out a little sob and laid her head on the steering wheel. After a moment, she lifted it. "You can talk to the dead. You did it at Astra's slumber party. You talked to Memaw. Can you still do it?"

"I mean, sure, but—"

"I don't need an explanation. I just needed to know you can do it." She put the car in reverse and pulled out of the parking space.

"Hold up! Where are you going?"

"We're gonna go talk to Nessa."

chapter
thirteen

"STOP THE CAR! I didn't say I'd go anywhere with you. Won't the police have your house cordoned off since the investigation is still ongoing?"

"This is Dead End, Star, not New York City. And besides, what they don't know..." She shrugged.

"I haven't talked to spirits in years, Jessi-Lyn." I pointed at my amulet. "There's a reason I have this."

"But you'll try." She didn't phrase it as a question.

If I backed out now, she might change her mind about letting Teeny and Kira see each other. I sighed. "Fine, let's just get this over with."

Jessi-Lyn lived in the historic district downtown. We could've walked, and driving took less than two minutes, so there wasn't much else said in the car.

We stepped through the front door, and I indicated

the area at the bottom of the wooden staircase. "Is that where her, uh...where you found her?"

Jessi-Lyn nodded, tears forming in her eyes. "Do you see her?"

I pulled the amulet over my head and carefully placed it on the entry hall table and suddenly felt naked, not just to my skin, but to my bones. I scanned the room but didn't see Nessa. There were a couple of other spirits. Judging by their clothing, they pre-dated the current house. I was careful not to make eye contact.

We made our way through each room on the bottom floor, then headed upstairs and finally found her in the last room we checked—Jessi-Lyn's bedroom.

I took a calming breath. "She's there, by the window."

"Does she look okay?"

"Yeah, I mean, they usually do. It's not like Beetlejuice or anything."

"What is she doing?"

"Nothing. Just standing there."

"Can she see me?" Jessi-Lyn waved her arms wildly, but Nessa didn't seem to notice.

I cleared my throat. "Nessa, Jessi-Lyn is here, and she has some questions for you."

"What'd she say?" Jessi-Lyn asked.

"Nothing yet. She's not talking." This was familiar territory, at least. It had been the same with Astra. I didn't know whether that made me feel better or worse. Perhaps it was only the newly dead who ignored me. But then, what did that mean for Astra now? Where was she, and why did she continue to ignore me? And her daughter.

"Nessa, honey! Talk to me!" Jessi-Lyn hollered at the curtains. Then to me, "You're not particularly good at this, are you? I don't know why you even came with me if you can't talk to the dead."

"You *kidnapped* me. I tried to warn you this could happen. It's not my fault she won't talk back. I don't even want to be here!"

"Neither do I!" Jessi-Lyn hollered and kicked over her vanity stool. "The love of my life is gone! She left me. And I didn't even get to say goodbye. Just like when my best friend died. I know you still blame me for Astra's death. I can see it in your eyes every time you look at me. And now I have no one."

She sat on the side of her bed.

"You have Kira." I ignored her comment about Astra. If I got into that right now, it wouldn't be pretty. "She loves you."

"I don't know why. I'm the worst mother in the world. And I think Kira knows it. That's why she spends so much time at Zeke's these days." Jessi-Lyn sniffed.

"Teeny doesn't seem to want to be around me either much. I know it's not the same because she's not my daughter, but I just think it's an age thing. Weren't you like that with your own mother?"

"Not really. I loved spending time with my mom. And now…I can't lose her on top of losing Nessa." Fresh tears fell then.

"Jess? Why are you crying?" Nessa spoke from behind me.

I whirled around. "Nessa?"

"Star? What are you doing here? Jess, what's going on?"

"You're dead." No time to be gentle. I needed to be efficient in case she suddenly faded away, like Astra had.

"She's talking to you now?" Jessi-Lyn stood up.

"Dead? I don't remember dying. And I don't feel dead."

"What's the last thing you remember?"

"I…I don't know. Jess?" Nessa said at the same time Jessi-Lyn asked, "What is she saying? Is she okay? No, of course she's not okay, she's dead. Can she hear me? Nessa, honey, can you hear me?" Jessi-Lyn shouted.

"Good grief, Jess! You don't have to scream. Yes, I can hear you. What's going on? Are you dead too? Why are we in your bedroom with Star?" She reached an arm toward Jessi-Lyn, but swiped air. Just like the living can't touch the dead, neither can they touch us.

Jessi-Lyn shot questions at me faster than a tommy gun and at the same time Nessa was hollering at Jess that she was standing right there in front of her. I stuck my fingers in my mouth and let out a sharp whistle. They both stopped and stared. "I can't hear either of you when you're both talking at once!"

I pointed to the bed and spoke to Jessi-Lyn, "You. Sit." Then to Nessa, "And you back up."

They both obeyed.

"Jessi-Lyn, let me talk to Nessa first, then I'll relay everything to you. And don't interrupt me, got it?"

She nodded.

"Nessa, what's the last thing you remember?"

She paced in front of the bed, never taking her eyes off Jessi-Lyn. "Labor Day weekend."

"Labor Day was over three weeks ago."

"Labor Day?" Jessi-Lyn seemed to grow even paler than she already was. "What does she remember about Labor Day?"

"We were on our way camping. We crossed over the bridge where Jess ...uh...the bridge over the lake."

Where Jessi-Lyn went over the bridge, taking my sister with her. That's what she didn't want to say. I relayed the last part to Jessi-Lyn. "The last thing she remembers is driving over the bridge to the lake."

"Nothing after that?" Jessi-Lyn asked, barely above a whisper.

Nessa said, "No, I don't even remember getting to the campground. I'm really dead?" Nessa stared at her hands as if the answer was there. "How?"

"Jessi-Lyn found you at the bottom of her staircase last night when she got home from the game."

"I fell?"

"We don't know. The police are investigating. Hold on so I can tell Jessi-Lyn all this before she explodes." I turned back to Jessi-Lyn. "She only remembers driving toward the campground. But not actually getting there."

Jessi-Lyn's shoulders slumped. "So, she doesn't remember our fight or our break-up."

"We broke up? Why in the world would we do that?" Nessa's face crumpled.

"No, she doesn't remember y'all breaking up. And she wants to know why." This felt like a conversation they should be having privately, but unfortunately, I was forced to play the part of Whoopi Goldberg in what felt like a crazy mixed-up revival of the movie Ghost.

"I..." Jessi-Lyn's face mirrored Nessa's.

"I can leave the room and she can still hear you. If you want to tell her privately," I offered.

Jessi-Lyn stared straight ahead and didn't say anything for a few moments. "I...I can't." Then sprang from the bed and ran from the room.

Nessa's eyes filled with tears, and she put her face in her hands. I don't know why it surprised me to see a spirit cry. I'd seen angry spirits. Spirits who laughed. Even indifferent spirits. So, of course, they could cry. But how the hell do you comfort a ghost? *There there, it's going to be okay. It's only death, it's not forever...* But before I could think of anything to say, Nessa faded away. Just like Astra had.

I was done. If Jessi-Lyn wouldn't take me back to the Merc, then I would walk. But it had been a long day, and I was done with all this. I went through the upstairs turning off all the lights that we'd turned on when looking for Nessa—because I'd been taught better than Jessi-Lyn—and I was just about to flip the switch of the one near the top step of the staircase when the front door opened and Detective Palmer stepped over the threshold.

chapter
fourteen

PALMER'S EYES widened in surprise, then annoyance crossed his face. "What are you doing here, Ms. Bell?"

I froze at the top of the stairs. "I'm here with Jessi-Lyn, we uh...came by to get some of her stuff."

He crossed the entry hall and stood at the bottom of the stairs. "You're trespassing and compromising evidence."

"I'm not," I insisted. "Ask her yourself."

"I would if she were here."

"Her car isn't outside?"

"No ma'am. And a neighbor reported the house lit up, and now it's dark again. So again, I'm asking you what you're doing here."

"First, she kidnaps me, then she leaves me here. Typical."

"Who kidnapped you?" Palmer stood against the post

at the bottom of the stairs wearing well-fitting jeans and a white button-down shirt.

"Jessi-Lyn."

He gave me a skeptical look.

I was about to argue back when the door opened again, and Carly stepped through. "I checked the perimeter, sir, and everything is secure."

Shock registered on her face when she saw me at the top of the stairs.

Palmer gave her a nod, then turned back to me. "Why don't you come on down now and tell me what's really going on?"

Carly gave me an exasperated look and mouthed, "What the hell?"

"I can explain everything." I took a step forward.

"Where's Jess? I think I remember something that might be relevant," Nessa said from behind me. "When we were at the lake."

I swung to face her. "What?"

"Ms. Bell?" Palmer asked. "What is it?"

"I...I...have to talk to Jessi-Lyn first," Nessa insisted.

"She's gone."

"Who is gone?" Palmer asked. His voice was closer now.

"Jessi-Lyn. She left." Then added for Nessa's benefit. "She drove off and left me here."

"Yes, Ms. Bell. You've established that."

I needed to get somewhere to talk to Nessa without Palmer there. I said over my shoulder, "I need to go to the bathroom."

"Stop right there. You're not going anywhere," Palmer insisted.

Nessa reached for me, and I backed up a step, but I was too slow because I felt her fingers clutch my shoulder and then I felt like I was falling. I grasped for something to hold on to. The banister. The wall. Anything. But there was nothing. I was going to die. I knew it as surely as I had known anything. My head hit the hardwood floor, and I heard a crunch. Everything started going black, and I fought it hard, but it overcame me.

Then I was walking through a parking lot at night. I could hear a phone ring, then someone picked up. "Kira's in bed and I have some Roscato chilling in the fridge. You on your way?"

"I can't make it tonight, babe. Krav Maga was rough, so I just came on home. I am exhausted. But how about we meet for breakfast?" I asked.

Or it wasn't me. I was someone else. I think.

"Nessa, you can't cancel on me again. What's going on? You're always gone. Is this about what happened at the lake?" Footsteps approached me from behind, and I whirled around and held a finger to my lips.

"No, Jess, I'm just exhausted. I'm gonna turn out the lights now and get some sleep. Talk to you tomorrow." I

clicked the red button and shoved my phone in my back pocket.

"All good?" The guy asked. I couldn't see his face because he stood in the shadows, but I felt like I trusted him.

"Yeah, Let's do this."

"Star!" Carly called from somewhere close by. "Are you okay?"

I opened my eyes then, and the bright light blinded me for a second. At least the pain in my head was gone, as was the dizziness. "I think so. What happened?"

"I don't know. It looked like you just fainted, and you almost fell backwards down the staircase, but Detective Palmer caught you."

I turned my head and found I was cradled in Palmer's arms. And we were on the stairs near the top, not at the bottom. I pushed myself into a sitting position and scooted to the next step but didn't stand yet. My legs felt like jelly. "I didn't fall down the stairs?"

Palmer stood and held out a hand to help me up, but I shook my head and managed it myself. What was all that I just experienced then? The falling? The parking lot? I rubbed the back of my head where I'd felt the pain before, but it wasn't tender at all. I swiveled my head, searching for Nessa, and she was gone again.

"No, honey," Carly said. "You almost did. But Detective Palmer sprang into action and caught you. I swear I've never seen anyone move so fast."

Palmer examined the top step. "I didn't notice it earlier, but this top step slanted. You probably stepped wrong and lost your balance. Old houses like this settle unevenly. You sure you're alright?"

I could still smell him and feel his warm skin on mine. I nodded. "Yeah, just shook up."

We descended the stairs and Palmer's face got serious again. "You said Jessi-Lyn was here with you? And that she kidnapped you?"

"I mean...not really. I could've left at any time. But she definitely got me into her car on false pretenses. She said she wanted to talk, then she brought me here."

"For what purpose?"

The front door opened yet again, and Jessi-Lyn stepped through. I don't know if Palmer and Carly parked further away or if Jessi-Lyn just didn't notice the patrol car because she seemed surprised when she saw them.

"Come on in, Ms. Gibson. Ms. Bell was just telling us how you kidnapped her and brought here even though you'd been asked to steer clear until we notified you, we were done here."

"I didn't kidnap her!" She shot me a look. "I needed some of my things and I didn't want to come here alone, so I brought Star with me."

"I wasn't aware you two were close." He kept his gaze on me but continued addressing Jessi-Lyn. "In fact, the things you said about Ms. Bell this morning, I'd have guessed you two were quite the opposite."

"Yeah, well, I'd just found my girlfriend dead at the bottom of the stairs, hadn't I? I wasn't in my right mind. The truth is, Star and I go way back. Her sister and I were best friends in high school."

"Where are your clothes?" Detective Palmer turned to Jessi-Lyn.

"What?" Jessi-Lyn replied.

"You said you were here to gather some of your things. Where are they?"

She shook her head. "I hadn't gotten them yet. Uh, that's why I came back."

He made a sweeping motion toward the stairs. "Go get them now. I don't want there to be any reason you need to come back here until I've cleared it. Deputy Davidson will accompany you. And Ms. Bell can keep me company."

Yay.

Once Jessi-Lyn and Carly headed up the stairs, Palmer turned his attention back on me. "So, would you like to tell me what was really going on up there? And who you were talking to?" Palmer asked.

"Nope."

"Excuse me?"

"You wouldn't believe me anyway."

"Try me."

"I was talking to Nessa," I said.

"Nessa? As in the deceased, Vanessa Anderson?" He shook his head. "What are you, a medium or something?"

I ignored both his comment and skeptical gaze. "Jessi-Lyn was upset and wanted me to unhex her, but when I told her I couldn't because I had never hexed her in the first place, she brought me here to talk to Nessa. To find out what happened to her."

He closed his eyes and shook his head. "And did she tell you how she died then?"

"No. She doesn't remember."

"Convenient." He ran a hand through his hair.

"I told you that you wouldn't believe me."

Carly and Jessi-Lyn returned then.

"Ms. Gibson, if you need anything else from your home before the scene is cleared, please call the station for an escort first. I would hate to have to arrest either of you," Detective Palmer gave me a pointed look, "for interfering with an investigation. Deputy Davidson will be patrolling the area all night just in case you think you can sneak back in."

He and Carly waited on the porch until we drove off. Carly gave me a look that meant I'd have to tell her everything, the real truth, later.

As soon as we got out of sight, she exploded. "You told him I kidnapped you? What the hell, Star."

"Well, you did! And then you left me there. What the hell, indeed!"

"Sorry. I was upset and needed some air."

We stayed silent the rest of the way to the Merc. I don't know what occupied Jessi-Lyn's mind, but I was trying to figure out my odd experience on the stairs. When we pulled in, I stepped out of the car and was halfway to the door when I stopped. I forgot to tell her about seeing Nessa again. But just as I opened my mouth I heard, "Carly said you nearly fell down the stairs?"

Jessi-Lyn sounded like she gave a care. A small one.

I stepped off the curb and went to the driver's side window. "Yeah. Nessa came back after you left. She was looking for you because she remembered something about the lake."

Jessi-Lyn's grip tightened on the steering wheel. "What did she remember?"

"She didn't say. She said she wanted to talk to you about it first." I hesitated to tell her about the parking lot, but she needed to know. "There was another vision. I saw her...no, that's not quite accurate. I *was* her, on the phone, telling you she couldn't make it to your house because she was tired. She lied. She was with someone she knew, and she didn't feel threatened or scared. Jessi-Lyn, she felt excited."

"Excited? About what?" She narrowed her eyes at me.

I shrugged. "I don't know. The vision ended there. You'd have to ask her yourself."

"And just how am I supposed to do that?"

Thankful I was already out of the car just in case she got any bright ideas about returning to her house, I said, "I don't know because I'm not going back. She grabbed my shoulder, and I blacked out. I could've died on those stairs, too."

"Well, you didn't, and my girlfriend did." Jessi-Lyn put her car in reverse and left me there without another word. Maybe I'd gone too far, but hopefully this would save her from going on a wild goose chase trying to find a murderer where there was none.

chapter
fifteen

THE PARADE WASN'T until ten in the morning, so I set my alarm as late as I could to still be able to make it to the beginning of the parade route in time to get into position on the float. We'd been at The Merc until well after midnight, but this year's float was sure to win first place. Our theme was The Nightmare Before Christmas. Sure, it was all still made from tissue paper flowers and chicken wire, but it was our best yet. A knock on my bedroom door woke me before the alarm went off and I hollered, "A thousand deaths to whoever is waking me up."

"You wouldn't kill your favorite aunt, would you?" Aunt Mer pushed open the door. She, of course, was fully dressed, hair done, and had full makeup on.

"No, but currently you're my least favorite." I wasn't kidding a bit. I loved sleep more than chocolate.

She crossed her arms over her chest. "I just didn't want you to oversleep. We've got to get there in time for Holly to do final touch ups on our costumes."

I reached for my phone to check the time but knocked it off the bedside table. "What time is it?"

"Almost seven."

"Almost? Gah, Aunt Mer. My alarm is set for seven fifteen. I could've gotten a few more minutes of sleep. And I'm Oogie Boogie; I don't need any touch ups. I'm basically wearing a potato sack."

She crossed my room and opened the curtains. "You're gonna turn into an Oogie Boogie if you don't come downstairs and have a decent breakfast. You know you get hangry when you don't eat."

"Yeah, and I get *slangry* when I don't get enough sleep." I had to get my own place soon. You can't complain about your aunt waking you up early when you're pushing forty and still living in her house.

"Star, it's too early in the morning for you to be making up words." Aunt Mer sighed.

"My point exactly." I sniffed the air. "Is there bacon?"

"I have two pounds I can fry, but you'd better get downstairs before Teeny mows through it. The early bird gets the bacon." She swatted my behind and left my room. Her mood had improved since last night—despite her frustration with me—and I wondered if that had anything to do with her and Uncle Gavin disappearing around the same time last night.

When I'd gotten back to the alley, I hadn't told anyone where I'd been. I wasn't sure they even missed me, or maybe Kira had told them. I stared at the ceiling and willed myself to get up, but last night's events lay heavily on my mind. What had happened at the top of the stairs? I needed to talk to Granny about it. This was a completely new ability. The vision, or whatever that was, had never happened before.

"Star! The bacon is disappearing faster than I can make it! You better get down here!" Aunt Mer hollered from the bottom of the stairs a few minutes later.

Teeny had in fact left me enough so that I wasn't surly. I sat at the table and made a bacon and jam sandwich with the toast and caught motion outside the window in the tree. Caroline. Son of buttered biscuit. I reached for my amulet and realized I'd left it upstairs. No. Not upstairs. At Jessi-Lyn's. I'd been so exhausted last night I hadn't realized I didn't have it on when I left.

Caroline waved enthusiastically. She'd been around since I was a child and was the one spirit who'd never asked anything from me. I waved back.

Teeny turned. "Who are you waving at?"

"Caroline. She's in the tree again."

"I thought Caroline was the old lady. What is she

doing up in the tree?" Teeny asked, then whipped around again.

"She's not old. I think she's around my age, I think. I don't know why she likes it up there." I got up and shut the curtains. I didn't like the way she sat and stared at us while we ate. Like a hungry puppy on the porch waiting to be let in.

We ate in relative silence with just a bit of small talk about the parade sprinkled in here and there, then Aunt Mer said, "We're gonna be late. I'll go start the car. Y'all just put the dishes in the sink, and we'll do them later.

"I'm gonna take my Jeep. I might go do something after the parade."

"Do *something*?"

"It's Dead Fest. There's lots to do. I just don't want to make you leave early or stay later if I don't want to." Plus, I needed to figure out how to get my amulet back without getting arrested.

"Do what you want, just hurry or you're gonna be late!"

As it turned out, Aunt Mer had been right. I managed to arrive and hop onto the trailer in full Oogie Boogie costume just as Zeke started the truck. Aunt Mer gave me a *told you so look* and handed me a bucket of candy to toss.

I positively vibrated with excitement as the truck

began to move. New York had its Thanksgiving parade, Boston had its St. Patrick's Day parade, and many small towns around us had impressive Christmas parades. But Dead End was becoming known for its epic Halloween parades. We'd even made it onto the Top Ten Must See Autumn Attractions in Texas list. People came from all around.

As we wound our way through the streets of downtown, I waved to the crowd and threw candy. I spotted so many familiar faces, and even more strangers. I wasn't sure if we had even more tourists this year or—I touched the bare spot between my collarbones—or if the extras were spirits. I needed to get my amulet back.

The last stop was in front of the Grand Marshall's podium. The Grand Marshall in past years was some resident of note appointed by the mayor. Granny was the Grand Marshall a few years ago, but ever since Hank Kendall was elected, he took the Grand Marshall position for himself. There he sat on the podium like a king with his court around him. His new wife, Mara, sat on one side and his son, Rowdy, on the other. I'd forgotten he was Mayor Kendall's son. When Rowdy was young, he got away with everything because his dad was a Deputy. He vandalized the school mascot but didn't get arrested because his dad was the one who showed up at the scene. The principal let him go home with him, the rumors said. Yeah, Holly dodged a bullet with that one.

And suddenly the parade was over almost as quickly as it had begun. Some might think all that work for a twenty-minute ride was a bit much, but it was worth every second to me. And one of the few days of the year I didn't work. This was my day.

I changed out of my costume and wove my way through the crowds toward the food booths. I spotted Grey standing near the corn dog stand with a drink carrier in one hand and two corn dogs in the other. He waved so hard he accidentally hurled one of the corn dogs across the path, nearly beaning a small child. The other dropped to the ground by his feet.

"Now you're throwing corn dogs at innocent children. Are you trying to get yourself fired, Mr. Principal?" I grinned.

"Hey, he looked hungry. Just thought I'd do him a solid." He winked at me and nodded to the line for Lemon Tree. "Wanna keep me company in line while I get replacement corn dogs?

I shrugged. "Sure."

We walked in awkward silence to the end of the line. I stared at my feet, trying not to notice any spirits. I didn't want whatever I experienced on the stairs to happen again. Then we both spoke at once.

"No hangover?" I asked.

"I heard you took me home last night?" he asked.

"Yeah, you don't remember that?"

"It's all fuzzy. Hope I didn't do or say anything I should regret."

"No, not at all. I think your reputation of upstanding school principal is preserved." I winked. "Although the neighbors called the cops on us when I tackled you."

He laughed. "That wasn't a dream? You really tackled me?"

"Yeah, because you wouldn't give me your house keys. You wanted to throw a rock through the window."

He shook his head. "So, did you put me to bed?"

"No, I was only able to get you as far as the sofa. Carly must have dragged you up to bed after I left."

"I heard she told you..."

"That you two are together? Yup. Congrats." I flashed a smile and hoped it looked more genuine than I felt. I would get used to the idea eventually, because I loved them both and wanted them to be happy.

"Wow, could you be a little less enthusiastic about it? I mean, you're killing me with all that joy."

"Sorry, I just... It's awkward, okay? It's just been the three of us for so long. Now it feels..."

"Like it's us against you?"

"Sorta."

"It's not, I promise. I mean Carly and I are an us, but you're not just a you because the three of us are still a we."

I snort laughed. "That probably made more sense in your head, I'm guessing."

His face relaxed. "Yeah, it did. What I'm trying to say is that this isn't going to change our friendship. The SGC lives on."

I grinned. We'd been *Stargate* fans in high school and into college (the tv show more than the movie) and because our initials just happened to be the same as "Star Gate Command," Grey called us the SGC. I didn't believe him that our friendship wouldn't change. It already had. But instead, I said, "I hope you're right. Where is Carly?"

"She's on her way. I hope. I got here early to save us a spot on the lawn and get our food. But she texted that she didn't get much sleep after she put me to bed. She had to work a double last night because of a couple of "idiots" she'd said tell me about later."

"Idiot number one at your service." I bowed dramatically and began relaying the previous night's events.

We reached the front of the line just as I got to the part about Palmer showing up. As Grey was placing his order, I spotted Carly a few feet away, having what looked like a heated discussion with Jessi-Lyn.

I left Grey in the line and strode over to them just in time to hear Carly say, "There's nothing I can do about it. The case is closed."

"Nessa's case? Why?" I asked.

"It was ruled an accident. The Sheriff is going to make a statement today," Carly explained.

"Accident, my ass!" Jessi-Lyn snapped.

"But there hasn't even been time for an autopsy, has there?" I asked.

"With it being ruled an accident, there won't be one unless her next of kin requests it," Carly said.

"Nessa had no living relatives. She only had me. I was her family. But Sheriff Briggs doesn't care about that. He gave me the same bull about it being an accidental death. She didn't fall," Jessi-Lyn insisted.

Carly laid her hand on Jessi-Lyn's arm. "The medical examiner agreed. Her injuries were consistent with a fall."

"Then the medical examiner is involved in the coverup!" Jess-Lyn jerked her arm away.

Grey showed up then with his Lemon Tree bounty. "What's going on?"

I shook my head, but the other two didn't even seem to notice his arrival.

"I know you're upset Jessi-Lyn, and I am sorry for your loss," Carly said. "But there's no cover up. Besides, the medical examiner was sent over from Travis County."

"Why Travis?" I asked.

"It's just how it's done. We don't have the budget for our own and we contract with Travis when we need to."

Jessi-Lyn's arm shot out and she pointed a finger at me. "This is your fault. If you hadn't been clumsy and fallen on the step last night, the detective wouldn't have gotten it into his head that my stairs are faulty. Kira and I walk up and down them several times a day and we never fall! Nessa was pushed."

"If the Sheriff thought there was any foul play, he wouldn't have closed the case. Trust me." Carly raised her voice this time.

Jessi-Lyn leaned in two inches from Carly's face. "No, *you* trust me. Nessa was murdered. And just because the Sheriff is your godfather or whatever, it doesn't mean he's a good cop. It's not like he's never gotten accused of wrongdoing before."

Grey and I exchanged just a brief glance before he shoved the food and drink carrier at me and grabbed Carly's hand. "Why don't you and I go somewhere and cool off? The sun is getting hot."

The sun wasn't the only thing on fire. Sheriff Briggs had stepped in to help take care of Carly's family after her dad died. Carly was super protective of him, and years ago there had been rumors of money going missing in a drug bust. Even though he'd been cleared, and the money was eventually found, she was still sensitive about it.

Carly jerked her hand away from him. "The Sheriff pulled your ass out of the lake."

Jessi-Lyn took a step back, but Carly took a step forward.

"He resuscitated you. If not for Paul Briggs, there would've been two dead girls in the lake that day. Don't you ever forget that Jessi-Lyn."

Jessi-Lyn turned without another word and scurried away. Carly stalked off in the opposite direction, with Grey close behind her. He shot me an apologetic look over his shoulder, but he was obviously choosing her over me, leaving me alone, just as I predicted they would.

chapter
sixteen

I **HAD** no clue what to do with the corn dogs and lemonade carrier, but as much trouble as Grey had gone through to get them; I wasn't about to dump them in the nearest dumpster. I headed toward the open green space in the middle of the town square—which never got renamed during the tourist boom and was unimaginatively named *The Square*—to see if I could find a seat. It was way too late to snag a prime spot, and everyone else had already started setting up chairs on the sidewalks and on the closed street, but I was hoping maybe I could squeeze in somewhere. And maybe even find someone to share the food with.

As luck would have it, I spotted Isaac and the boys and waved. I pointed at the corn dogs, but right before I did, Isaac turned to attend to Fox and didn't see me. Instead, Detective Palmer—who was also in my line of sight—squinted at me and awkwardly returned my wave, then stood and pointed to the open spot on his blanket. Awesome.

I thought about pretending I didn't see him and taking the long way around to Isaac and the boys. Or I could use this opportunity to pick his brain about why the case was closed. I wound my way through the many blankets and lawn chairs and had the sudden horrible thought that maybe he was also waving at someone behind me.

Palmer wiped his hands on his jeans when I approached. "Right after I waved back, I realized you were probably waving at someone behind me."

I laughed and it wasn't even forced. "I was, but I feel like we got off on the wrong foot last night and you did save my life, after all."

He rubbed the back of his neck. "Anyone would've done the same."

"So," I nodded to a corn dog, "I have all this extra food that is probably already cold, but would you like the world's best corn dog and lemonade?"

The small talk while we ate pretty much stayed on safe subjects like the weather, the crowds, and the food that he agreed was excellent. I was trying to find a way to bring up the case when the mic on stage went hot and screeched at us. I turned to the stage in anticipation of the concert starting, but instead of the band behind the mic, it was the mayor.

"We suffered a tragic loss yesterday of a beloved coach and teacher from our own Dead End High School. Vanessa Anderson had been with the school for almost a decade and coached the girls' volleyball team to the state championship three years in a row. And while we've lost our friend, teacher, and co-worker too soon, the rumors circulating that it was a homicide are completely untrue. I'm going to turn it over to our own Sheriff Briggs, now for a statement."

Sheriff Briggs regurgitated what the mayor had said and added that after a careful review of the evidence, they'd found Coach Anderson's death had been nothing but a tragic accident.

The mayor took over again and assured the audience the town was safe. And *when* he was reelected, he would continue to ensure our safety. It was clear the band's opening act was the mayor's campaign rally, and it sounded like it might go on for a while.

"See you later." I grabbed our empty cups and assorted trash and stood. I slowly wound my way through the crowds on the lawn. With the living and dead, it took a while. I should be happy Nessa's death had been ruled an accident since it let Teeny off the hook, and it also meant there wasn't a murderer running loose in Dead End. But after Jessi-Lyn and Carly's fight, something felt off. Why was the case closed so suddenly? I stopped in my tracks. And why was Nessa even at Jessi-Lyn's house since they'd broken up? No one had asked that.

"You're deep in thought," a voice said behind me. "Did you lose something? Maybe your purse?"

I turned around and found Palmer holding my handbag and his blanket.

"I just couldn't sit there and listen to him drone on like he was Dead End's savior or something. And now you've lost your spot on the lawn. I'm sorry."

He rubbed the back of his neck. "Well, to tell you the truth, I wasn't sure how much longer I was going to be able to sit there and listen to his voice either. Someone needs to give the guy a throat lozenge."

I raised my eyebrows. I figured he'd defend the mayor as a fellow public servant. I tested the waters. "You believe it was an accident? Like they are claiming? I'm not sure I buy that."

"Don't buy that it was an accident or don't buy that I'm on board with that theory."

"Both." It didn't slip past me he called it a theory. Was he having doubts, too?

The mayor's microphone screeched again.

"Let's walk." Palmer cocked his head in the opposite direction of The Square and once we'd gotten far enough away, he said, "If I didn't believe the truth had been discovered, I wouldn't stop until it was."

"You were pretty sure it was a murder yesterday morning when you dragged me out of bed and interrogated my niece. What changed between then and now?"

"I never said it was murder then either, Ms. Bell. Your niece was the one who called it that. I called it what it was, a suspicious death."

"And how is a suspicious death not a murder, Detective?"

He gave me the tolerant look you'd give a toddler when they asked why they had to eat their *betchtables*. "A suspicious death can be any that is unattended, among other criteria. It is a suspicious death until the evidence shows the cause. I was still gathering evidence. You and your niece were part of that because she was seen crawling out of an upstairs window at night."

"And last night when you ripped me a new one for trespassing at a crime scene. What was that all about?"

"Ripped you a...?" He shook his head. "I saved your life, as you pointed out earlier, Ms. Bell."

"Yes, you saved my life, and I thanked you with corn dogs and lemonade."

"And those were damn good corn dogs and lemonade." He said with gravity, but I could swear a small smile danced on the edge of his lips, begging to come out and play. I willed it not to because I did not want to like this man. At all. And I was in no mood for jokes.

"But why was everything done so quickly? She died

yesterday and today the case is closed. There wasn't even time for an autopsy."

Palmer scratched the side of his beard. "This isn't a TV crime show, Ms. Bell. Autopsies cost taxpayer dollars and are only performed when the medical examiner deems it necessary, and he didn't. He gave me his findings, which I can't discuss with a civilian. But just trust me when I say that if I believed anything criminal happened, you can believe I'd be investigating."

I studied his face. He seemed to be sincere. I nodded, then turned to go.

"Hold up," Palmer said.

"What?"

He held out my purse and I took it from him.

"Thanks for catching me when I fell last night."

"Anytime."

Jessi-Lyn's house was within walking distance of downtown. Her car sat in the driveway and Jessi-Lyn lay draped across the steering wheel, completely still. I jerked open the door, ready to perform CPR, when she lifted her head and glared at me. "What the hell, Star?"

"Sorry, I thought...never mind. Are you okay?"

"No, Star. I'm not. I don't think I ever will be again." She stared toward the front door. "They said I can go back in, but I don't think I can."

I knew in my heart the pain she was going through, while not completely the same since I'd lost a sister, not someone I was in love with. And I hadn't found Astra's body—no one had because the lake claimed her forever. But I knew loss. And I knew there was nothing I could do or say that would make it better. Nothing she could do to make the pain ever go away. It would disappear at times, briefly, but then it would come rushing back and she'd feel like she was drowning in the pain all over again.

Jessi-Lyn met my eyes. "They said she had sleeping meds in her system, the kind that really makes you loopy and that she must have tripped and fallen. But it doesn't make sense. Nessa hates drugs, and I could never even get her to take something for a headache. They're all in the mayor's pocket and covering up the fact that Nessa was murdered."

"Could it be incompetence rather than a cover-up, Jessi-Lyn?"

She snorted and mumbled, "sure."

"But why would they cover it up? Do you think the mayor had something to do with it personally?" I asked. "Did he even know Nessa?"

"No, he's covering for his son."

"Rowdy? What does he have to do with Nessa?"

"She cheated on me. With him. That's why we broke up," she said.

I thought about Holly saying she saw Nessa's name

pop up on Rowdy's phone. So, I had little doubt she was right about that part. "But why would he kill her?"

"Who knows what's in the mind of a psychopath, Star!" Her bite was back. I supposed that was a good sign.

"No, I mean, just because they were together, what makes you think it would turn violent?"

"Because he threatened her. I found them in the bar together, cozied up in a booth in the back, sitting side by side and talking in low voices. She used that trite excuse of 'It's not what it looks like, Jess, I promise!' I stormed out and she followed me, and he followed her. He threatened her that if she talked, then she was going to die. Then he jumped in his truck and drove off."

The Rowdy I had known was mischievous, not violent, but I hadn't been around him since he was a kid. He'd gone off after high school and joined the military and had only come back to town recently. Who knew what kind of man he'd become. And I could totally get on board with his dad helping to cover things up, but he'd have to have the Sheriff on board to do that, wouldn't he? I'd known Bill Briggs my whole life. He'd been at every one of Carly's birthday parties, and I'd even stayed overnight at his house a few times with Carly. Was Jessi-Lyn being dramatic? Or was there something to it? I thought about the vision on the stairs when I fell. Nessa was excited. Not scared. "Did you ask Nessa what she was doing at the bar with Rowdy?"

Jessi-Lyn opened her mouth and closed it again. She made a dismissive motion with her hand. "We'll never know the truth of that, will we?"

I gestured to the house. "If she's in there, she can tell us."

She glanced sharply at me. "I thought you said you never wanted to go back in there. Besides, you said she said she didn't remember anything past Labor Day."

"Right, but if she was cheating on you with him, maybe it started before then?"

She stepped out of her car and slammed the door behind her. "It doesn't matter. I just want to go crawl into my bed and forget for a while."

Jessi-Lyn disappeared into her house without another word. Leaving me wondering if she was afraid of what Nessa might say, or what she might say to me.

BY THE TIME I'd gotten back downtown, the festivities were winding down for the day and folks were closing their booths. The only thing left was the street dance, and I didn't feel much like dancing.

Instead, I sat at the stop sign at the end of our road and flipped my blinker to the right toward the graveyard. Jessi-Lyn's grief had brought back the pain of Astra's death and the devastation of her not talking to me. I needed her now more than ever. And maybe that's what it took. Maybe me needing her enough would help me find her. Miracles happen in the movies all the time, right? But at the last second, I turned the wheel and headed home instead.

Aunt Mer's car wasn't in the driveway. They were probably still at the street dance. Aunt Mer loved nothing more than the Two Step. I was thankful for the alone time. Caroline sat in her second favorite spot, the porch swing. She waved and opened her mouth to speak, but I held up a hand and shook my head. Why was it this one ghost was everywhere and talked my ear off, but the ghosts I wanted to talk to were AWOL? I didn't want to listen to Caroline's chatter. I wanted to talk to my sister, find Nessa, or if none of those were options, at least fall face first into my bed and sleep for twelve hours or more. And now that I didn't have to play Nancy Drew to clear Teeny's name, I didn't have to talk to the ghosts either.

"So there!" I said aloud to no one in particular.

I pulled out my keys to unlock the door and dropped them. They fell between the wooden boards into the crawlspace below. They weren't gone forever but would take some effort to retrieve them. It was the proverbial straw. I let out a primal scream and dropped to the steps.

"Oh dear," Caroline said and sank to the steps beside me.

I no longer had it in me to fight, so I didn't tell her to go away and leave me alone and instead buried my face in my hands.

I felt her wrap her arms around me and suddenly I was struggling to stay awake, and I could feel a hard surface beneath my back, but that wasn't right. I had to be sitting up because I still felt her arms around me, but suddenly it was bright too, with interspersed moments of darkness as if I was opening my eyes to a bright room. *Shapes in white stood above me and people spoke in low voices. It sounded like someone said, "She's asleep. Let's begin." My eyelids were so heavy, and I couldn't fight it, but found I didn't want to. I closed my eyes and let the waves of sleep carry me away.*

"Honey? Star! Wake up. I brought the doctor!" Caroline's face came into view, fuzzy at first, but sure enough, it was her standing over me with a man dressed in overalls.

"I'm Dr. Levi. How are you feeling, miss?"

"I think I'm okay." I sat up and found I was still on the steps, and it was pitch black all around us except for the porch light casting a glow. "What happened?"

Caroline wrung her hands. "I wrapped my arms around you, and I thought I'd killed you. It was like you fainted or something. But I couldn't wake you up, so I ran for the doctor."

"I thought you couldn't leave the property?"

"Why ever would you think that?" Caroline asked.

"Because you're always here."

"Because it's where I am happiest." She put her hands on her hips and turned to look at the house. "My Daddy built this house. Long before the Bells moved in."

I studied the man. He didn't look like a doctor. He looked like a farmer. All he needed was a pitchfork in his hand and he could've been the guy from the *American Gothic* painting. "And you? Where do you live…I mean, where are you…the happiest?"

A brief shadow crossed his face, then he stood up straight and said, "I have the farm over by the cemetery, but my great-grandson Gavin—never got to meet him…before—grows lavender there. I think he does fairly well with it. He's a good kid. Looks a lot like my wife, Sarah."

This was Uncle Gavin's great-grandfather. I'd have to tell him some time I'd met his ancestor and pass along the compliment. But for now, something was niggling at the back of my brain.

"Caroline, why did you run for the doctor? What happened?"

"You slumped over on the porch steps. I thought you'd died. It's foolish now when I think of it. I don't know what I thought the doctor could do for you. But I panicked. And I'm so sorry, honey. I didn't know it was harmful touch the living. Did you, Dr. Levi?"

The doctor said, "I've never met a living who could see me, so I mean, I guess I never even thought about touching them."

That's what was hiding on the edges of my mind. Before Nessa, and now Caroline, I had been so careful to not let a spirit touch me. I'd brushed into a few before and it made me dizzy, which is one of the reasons I wear the amulet, but is that what triggered these death visions? They had to touch me. With intent. Not just accidentally. But it was different this time. I didn't feel like I was falling. I felt peaceful. I cast a glance at the doctor. He had kind eyes. I'd seen them before. Maybe it was because Uncle Gavin was his great-grandson. "So, you two knew each other when you were alive?"

"Oh, yes, he was my doctor. He was treating me for things a lady shouldn't really mention to folks other than her physician. He wanted to do an operation, but my husband didn't want me to have it." Her hands rested near her abdomen, and she turned to Dr. Levi. "I hope you're not still upset about that. It's not that Johnny didn't trust you. He was just so scared of losing me."

"And he never forgave me, I'm afraid."

"Forgave you. Whatever for?"

"You don't remember? You had the surgery after all, and you died on my table."

She sat on the step. "No, I don't remember. I remember leaving your office after telling you I wouldn't be having the surgery and...I don't remember much after that. Why don't I remember?"

"You don't remember coming back a few days later and telling me you changed your mind?" He asked.

Caroline shook her head.

He placed a finger over his lip and looked up. "You left

my office on a Friday afternoon like you said and told me you wouldn't have the operation. Then on Monday you came back and told me you'd changed your mind because you'd had a lot of bleeding over the weekend. You asked me if I could guarantee you the pain and bleeding would go away and I explained that yes, without a womb, there would be no place for the—"

"Hush, I don't need the specifics of it. I'm sure it was horrid enough hearing about it the first time. So, you did the procedure, and I died? Oh, my poor Johnny."

Dr. Levi placed a hand on her arm. "He was devastated. I don't think he ever forgave me."

I had a sudden clarifying thought. "When you operated on her, were you wearing white?"

"Yes, I mean, that's what we wore for surgical procedures."

"I lived her death."

"You did what?"

"When you touched me, I felt very sleepy. I saw people in white standing over me and someone said, 'She's asleep. We can start now. You said she died on the table.'"

He nodded solemnly.

"I felt peaceful and safe because that is the last thing Caroline felt."

The doctor's eyes filled with tears, and he disappeared right before our eyes, like Nessa had done.

"Honey, I think I need to go lie down if you'll excuse

me." Caroline vanished as well. I absently wondered where ghosts go to lie down, especially since there were wards on the house. But I dismissed those thoughts, as I had something way more important to consider. I felt Nessa's death. I was pushed. Was Jessi-Lyn right? Was Nessa murdered? I needed to talk to Carly.

chapter
eighteen

THE STREET DANCE was in full swing by the time I retrieved my keys from underneath the porch and drove back downtown. I could hear the music before I even stepped out of my Jeep. I scanned the crowds for Carly.

Many familiar faces swung by under the lights. Aunt Mer and Uncle Gavin. Aunt Willa Jo was on the dance floor with Isaac and even Aunt Tatty and Granny were there, both in their scooters on the sidewalk. I was glad to see Granny downstairs.

Zeke danced with Kira, but she looked like she'd rather be anywhere else.

"How can adults be so blind?" Teeny said next to me.

"Oh, hey, there you are!" I slung an arm around her and squeezed.

She shrugged me off and crossed her arms over her chest. "Why are we still having this dance?"

"People grieve in different ways, honey."

"I get that but let us grieve the way we want. Don't force us out on the dance floor!" She flung her arm toward Kira.

"She didn't want to dance with her father?"

"No, she's only out there to make him happy. She'd do anything to make him happy."

"Okay, this is one thing I can fix." I kissed Teeny on the forehead and strode out onto the dance floor. I tapped Kira on the shoulder and said, "Could I cut in?"

"Please do!" She was off the floor quicker than it took Zeke to take me in his arms.

"Star, I didn't know you cared." Zeke winked. And we fell into the rhythm of the two-step.

"I'm not doing this because I want to. I'm on a mission."

"Oh, you're using me? I am intrigued." He winked and spun me around. "What's up?"

"Kira looked miserable and Teeny was worried about her." I wasn't ready to fill him in on my suspicions. I had to keep my eyes open for Carly.

"I'm not clueless. I know she didn't want to be out here with her dad, but I too am on a mission. She has a lot on her mind, and I was trying to distract her. Her mother can't be bothered."

"Yeah, well, leave that to Teeny. And Kira's mother is

grieving. She's lost the only person she's ever been in love with."

"Ouch."

I swatted his chest. "Don't give me that fake pain. You were never in love with Jessi-Lyn. You married her out of duty."

He snorted. "That was probably the biggest mistake I made in my life, but I don't regret the results."

"Kira is a pretty good kid."

"Yeah, she is. I can't imagine my life without Kira, but sometimes I wonder where I would've ended up if Jessi-Lyn hadn't gotten pregnant."

"You." I poked him in the chest. "Would still be breaking hearts all across Texas."

"Maybe. Or just maybe I'd have been happy with what I'd found and finally settled down."

"With what you found?"

Zeke seemed to be someplace else. Or some other time. He said in a faraway voice, "I'd found someone. Someone I really cared about, and I think she might have started to care for me, but I had to go and screw it up. I've been paying for it since then." He spun me again, and the song ended and so did the spell he'd woven with his voice.

I had to shake my head to snap out of it.

"I think I might take Kira to get ice cream if she wants to. Is it okay if Teeny comes with us?" he asked.

"Sure, just have her let Aunt Mer know where she is."

"You wanna come too?"

I did, but I spotted Carly just then. "No. I have something I need to do."

She was still in uniform and stood over on the sidewalk in front of the bank, scanning the crowds. She gave me a small, tired smile when she saw me. "Hey, I haven't seen you much tonight. Where'd you get off to?"

I didn't point out that she was the one who abandoned me after her and Jessi-Lyn's fight. "That's what I want to talk to you about. You still on duty?"

"Yeah, but I can take a break." She spoke into her radio, then to me said, "Let's walk down to the gas station on the corner. I've been dying for a cold drink. And to vent to you about Jessi-Lyn's shenanigans. I've always supported you in your dislike for her, but man, now I really get it. Can you believe the nerve of her? Bringing up the past like that? Not to mention accusing my godfather of covering up a murder."

The sidewalk was mostly deserted, with most people in the square. I said, "That's kind of what I want to talk to you about. You know that night I fell on the stairs?"

"Exactly! You falling and almost dying on her stupid crooked stairs should prove to her it was an accident."

"But I don't think it was, Carly. Just listen to me for a minute."

I told her about the vision I had. And then what happened with Caroline and the doctor. "I don't think Nessa fell. She was pushed. These visions prove it."

"Are you kidding me with this? You of all people, Star. I cannot believe you are taking Jessi-Lyn's side. She is the reason your sister is dead." Carly paced.

"You don't have to remind me of that. I live with it every single day." I glared at her.

She returned the intensity of my gaze for a beat, then when she spoke, her voice was softer. "I know. I'm sorry. It's just…I've always envied you for having this special power, but right now all I can think of is how the hell do you manage to form complete sentences with everything you are going through that we can't see. And now you're just inviting more stress into your life by going along with Jessi-Lyn's wild imagination? Girl."

"I don't *invite* stress into my life. I didn't ask Jessi-Lyn to kidnap me. I didn't ask Nessa to grab me. But these visions are real. They came from me. Not Jessi-Lyn."

"Okay, but Uncle Paul isn't the bad guy here." She crossed her arms over her chest and stared at me like she dared me to contradict her.

Dare taken. "Carly, I know what he means to you, and I know what he did for you after your dad died, but good people can do bad things under the right pressure."

"Not Uncle Paul."

"So, you believe in him, but not me?"

"It's not like that, Star. You say you felt Nessa being pushed? Fine. I believe you. But there is no cover up."

I sighed. There would be no arguing with Carly and no help from her on this. I was on my own. She lives up to every description of her Taurus birth sign. She wouldn't be moved once she made up her mind. It's a great thing when she's on your side fighting for you, but on the opposite side, she was like trying to move a truck with its parking brakes on, up a hill, with your baby toe. I needed to try a different tack. "Okay, so what happens if we are both right? Let's say you are one hundred percent correct and there was absolutely no cover-up, and I'm one hundred percent correct Nessa was pushed. That means something was overlooked. And I know the mayor has the department busy with crowd-control for the festival, so what would it hurt for me to look into things?" I held my hands palm up in front of me.

"How exactly are you going to *look into things*?" she asked.

"I'm going to start with Rowdy."

"Star."

"Jessi-Lyn caught him and Nessa together at a bar. And Holly said messages were coming in on his phone from Nessa.

Her radio crackled then, and she said to me, "I have to go. You're not going to do anything stupid, right?"

"Nope. I promise." I was going to be smart about my next move.

I knew Rowdy had to be here somewhere if he was on duty tonight. The mayor was putting on a show of strength by putting cops everywhere for his campaign platform of keeping Dead End safe. After about twenty minutes, I spotted Rowdy on the other side of the square. He was also in uniform talking with another cop I recognized by face—but not the name—from the time I'd been Carly's plus one at a department picnic. I headed his way, grabbing an empty red cup and pretended to drink it as I stumbled toward him.

"Rowdy Kendall, is that you? Damn, you're even more drunk when I'm hot!" I slurred my words. "I mean, hot...drunk. Whatever."

The other cop said something in a low tone, grinned, and slapped Rowdy on the back as I approached.

"Hey, Star. You okay there?" Rowdy stepped forward to steady me.

"I'm great." I grabbed his hand and pulled him back. "You owe me a dance for all the crap you put me through at summer camp."

Color flooded his face. Whether that was a show, or whether he was really embarrassed about his past self, I didn't know. But that didn't mean he was innocent now.

He gave me a small, sad smile. "I was really that bad, huh?"

I said, "You were, but it seems time has changed you."

His face transformed then. The mask was off, and storms raged on his face. "No, it really hasn't."

"You're a cop now. One of the good guys."

He snorted. "Yeah, a real white hat wearing good ole boy."

The other cop tipped his cowboy hat at me. "Here to serve and protect."

And then I felt things going dark as if someone dimmed the lights.

I was Nessa again in the parking lot. Except this time, I turned and saw the person who was behind me. It was Rowdy. And then I was driving down a narrow dark dirt road. I was alone in the car but following another vehicle closely. It was a truck. A large one. The license plate read RWDY1. I felt excited. And determined. But then I felt a tug on my arm, and I was in the parking lot again. Not the same one. This one contained only a couple of vehicles, but mostly motorcycles. The biker bar Jessi-Lyn mentioned.

"Nessa, stop," Rowdy pleaded.

"I have to tell her," I said.

"No way in hell, Nessa. You do that and you may as well start planning your funeral because you're dead. You feel me?"

I turned back and looked over my shoulder. Jessi-Lyn

was almost to her car, which was parked beside Rowdy's truck. I jogged over to her to stop her from leaving before I could explain. I heard the crunch of gravel behind me as Rowdy chased after me.

Rowdy grabbed my arm just as I reached Jessi-Lyn. "Please don't. It's a dangerous game you're playing with this whole thing here. Just think before you talk to her, okay? I like you too much to see you dead."

And then my vision cleared, and Rowdy was holding onto me, looking concerned.

"You threatened her," I said.

"What?"

"You said if she told Jessi-Lyn she was going to die? And then she died."

"How much did you have to drink?" He glanced at the other cop and grinned, but the mask was off. "Why don't I escort you home?"

"No, I'm—"

"Hanson, I'll be back in a bit." Rowdy nodded to the other cop and took my arm gently, but firmly. He hissed in my ear, "Don't make me arrest you."

As soon as we got out of sight, he let go and leaned down a couple of inches from my face. "I don't know what you're playing at, pretending to be drunk, but you're gonna get hurt if you go around saying stuff like that. I like you. You never yelled at me like the other camp counselors. I wouldn't want you to get hurt. So, drop it. You feel me?"

He stormed off the street and disappeared into the crowd, leaving me standing there looking and feeling like a fool and shaking slightly.

BREAKFAST the next morning was a quiet affair. At least on Teeny and Aunt Mer's side of the table. Something was off. Sunday brunch usually contained a big spread, and Uncle Gavin was sometimes invited, but this morning Teeny scarfed down a bowl of cereal and Aunt Mer only sat staring at an empty coffee cup.

"Y'all are all doom and gloom this morning." I pushed the curtain above the sink as far back as it would go and opened the window. Last night scared me, but it didn't scare me away. It had only made me more determined, and I would just be more careful in my investigating.

Aunt Mer blinked and shielded her eyes like a vampire whose coffin had been opened before sunset. She nodded toward the open window. "And you are much too cheery this morning."

"Caroline is in the tree, and I thought it would be nice

to include her in our breakfast." After our conversation last night, I decided I was going to be nicer to her.

"Good morning, Merilee, Teeny." Caroline waved, but my two unseeing companions just stared past her.

"Caroline is waving at you."

They both waved back but didn't put a bit of heart into it.

"You'll have to excuse their lack of manners, Caroline. They were up late and at least one of them is hung over," I joked.

"I'm not hung over," Aunt Mer insisted.

"She's right." Caroline said. "She and the Bright boy got into a fight last night."

I raised my eyebrows. I'd have to pump Caroline later for more information about that, but for now nodded at Teeny. "And that one. What's her deal?"

"Don't discuss me with your imaginary friends, Star," Teeny said.

"Friends? She called me your friend," Caroline said and clasped her hands together. "The little one. I don't know why she's upset. She was happy enough last night when she came in."

"Oh, really?" I glanced at Teeny.

"Someone woke up on the right side of the bed for once," Aunt Merilee commented when I sat a hot cup of coffee and the half and half in front of her. "Does that have anything to do with you cozying up to Detective Palmer on a picnic blanket yesterday?"

Teeny's head shot up.

"No, and I wasn't cozying. I was pumping him for information."

"Is that what the kids are calling it these days?" Aunt Mer made kissing noises.

Teeny threw a wadded-up napkin at her. "Gross!"

I didn't have a chance to tell her my theory because the phone rang. The house phone could only mean one thing.

We all stared at the phone, none of us moving. It was a mental game of chicken, and I could guarantee you I wasn't going to lose this one.

Aunt Mer sighed and scooted her chair back but shot me a frustrated look. "Hello?"

My mother's voice—drifted isn't strong enough—assaulted us from the receiver. Aunt Mer held the phone a few inches away from her ear to protect her own eardrums.

"Tell me again why we still have a landline?" Teeny asked. "Why doesn't she text like a normal person?"

I ignored her so I could hear what my mother was saying. It wouldn't have been that hard, except Caroline had also picked that time to offer her own observations. "Is that Ruby Dee? She was such a beautiful thing. Why doesn't she ever come back and visit?"

"Why indeed."

Teeny took this as an answer to her question and went back to her cereal. I heard my name and then Aunt Mer said, "Sure, hold on."

I shook my head vehemently and mouthed, "No, I'm in the shower."

Aunt Mer hooked the receiver on my shoulder and said, "Be nice."

I closed my eyes as if that would give me strength and put the phone to my ear. "Hey Mamma."

There was no "Hey baby" or "Hey darling" like Isaac and Holly got from Aunt Willa Jo even after she'd been away from them for only a few hours. Instead, she skipped the greeting altogether and got straight to the point. "Have you talked to Daisy lately?"

"I haven't."

"When she calls you, you need to keep an open mind."

"About what?" I asked. Although I didn't think I wanted to know the answer to that.

"Just give her a chance, Star. She really wants—" She must have put her hand over the receiver because I heard her raise her voice at someone else, but it was muffled. Then louder as she finished with, "I said I'm on my way."

"Sounds like you're busy, Mamma, I'll just let you go."

"No, wait, let me finish. You've lost one sister. Don't push Daisy away too. Now, put Mer back on the phone."

I swallowed down all the hateful but justified words that threatened to burst forth and wondered, not for the first time, why Mamma hadn't just used birth control instead of bringing a child into the world she obviously didn't like. But instead, I said, "Your granddaughter is here. Wouldn't you like to talk to her?"

Teeny's eyes grew wide, and she shook her head so hard I thought it would spin right off.

Mamma gave a dramatic sigh. "I have to get to rehearsal. Fine, just for a minute."

I handed the phone to Teeny, who shot daggers at me with her eyes. In a flat tone and without taking a breath, she said, "I'm great. My teacher was murdered, and the police thought I hexed her to death and even though it's been ruled an accident, the kids at school look at me like I'm Hannibal Lecter, so it's all sunshine and ponies here. Great talk. Bye now."

She hung up the phone and glared at me.

Aunt Mer's phone buzzed then, and she glanced at it. "No school tomorrow, instead there will be a memorial for Coach Anderson in the gym."

We both looked to Teeny expectantly. She hadn't mentioned Nessa since yesterday. But she only shrugged and said, "See, even my school knows texts are more efficient than phone calls."

chapter
twenty

I ROLLED into work around eleven. I would've been there earlier but had to park in the overflow parking lot and take the shuttle to Main Street. It would be like this for the rest of the month, so I might as well get used to it. At least it let up a bit during the weekdays, but weekends were another thing.

I threw my stuff into my locker, put on my apron, and was behind the bar within ninety seconds of stepping through the door. I barely said much more than hi, or behind you, to Zeke and the other servers over the next few hours. When it finally did slow down, I found Zeke in Boone's office doing paperwork. Boone had been gone a bit over a month and none of us had any clue when he was returning, so it was up to Zeke to run things, which included making the schedule.

I poked my head through the door. "I hope my cousin is paying you well for all of this extra work."

"I live rent free, eat all my meals free, and get a decent wage, so no need for any extra pay. And I enjoy what I do. Except for scheduling." He shook a paper at me. "It's like the worst math problem ever. Jenna can only work mornings, Tammy can only work evenings, Matt can work any hours, but has a romantic history—his words—with both Jenna and Tammy so I can't schedule him when either of them are working. Frank prefers to work behind the bar, but he's a terrible bartender."

I stepped into the office and sat in the chair beside his desk, closing the door behind me. "And Star? What's that girl's problem?"

"She works too much and doesn't clock in for half those hours." He raised his eyebrows at me. "I saw you here every day last week, yet your timecard only shows twenty-two hours."

I shrugged. "Family helps family. But speaking of that, I am going to take a couple of days off this week."

"Good girl! Doing anything fun?"

"Oh, just the usual. Netflix binge, brunch with friends, trying to solve a murder."

He lowered his voice. "Please tell me you're not getting involved in Nessa's death, Star."

"Nessa's *murder*. I already have. And it's not going so

great." I confided in him about my suspicions, including talking to Nessa, falling on the stairs, and my visions.

Zeke leaned back in his chair and clasped his hands behind his head. "You have to be careful. You could've died on those stairs like Nessa. And if she was murdered and the wrong people know you're snooping around in this, whoever killed Nessa could come after you next."

"I know. You don't have to lecture me. I'm aware that I have no business trying to solve a murder. I don't know what the crap I'm doing. Hell, I was shocked every time they unmasked the bad guy in Scooby Doo."

The lines in his face eased, and a grin curled his lips. He said in a raspy voice, "And I woulda gotten away with it if it wasn't for you meddlesome kids and your mangy mutt."

"I don't think that's the right line."

"How would you know? You didn't even know it was Mr. Jenkins behind the mask the whole time." He leaned forward. "So why are you doing it if you know you're out of your league?"

"Thanks for the support."

"No, I mean, why *you*? You had no real ties to Nessa."

"Because I'm the only one who can talk to ghosts. They are the silent witnesses." They hadn't been all that helpful so far, though. "And because I know what it feels like to lose someone and not know why."

He nodded. "There it is. This is about Astra, isn't it?"

"Isn't everything?" I sighed.

Emotion clouded his eyes. He knew. He'd been there with me that day. The day when Astra left me for good.

"What does she say about all of this mess?"

I teared up but didn't let them fall down my face. I did the hand wave thing that we always think is going to magically stop the tears, but never does. I let a few tears fall and took the tissue Zeke handed me. After a moment. I took a deep breath and began, "Astra is the only spirit I can't see."

He took both his hands in mine. "Seriously? Why?"

I shrugged. "I'm pretty sure she's hiding on purpose."

"That doesn't sound like her at all."

"Yeah, well, I never thought she'd leave me here to go live with our mother, either."

Zeke was silent for a few moments, then said, "What happened between the two of you? You two were always so close."

Zeke and I had been friends for years, but we never talked about Astra or that day. We'd been hanging out at the diner—we hadn't become friends yet, just victims of circumstance—sharing a plate of fries when a lady burst through the door saying Jessi-Lyn's car had just gone off the bridge. But talking about Astra now felt right. He'd been there to witness my pain when they pulled only one person out of the lake. "I don't know if you remember when she left town suddenly. She said she wanted to go live with our mom in Nashville. She said she felt like she should give Mamma a chance. We got into a huge fight, and I told her she was abandoning me just like Mamma did to both of us."

"How did she respond to that?"

"She barely kept in touch with me the whole time she was gone but called on my birthday. She said she wanted to talk to me about something, but just a few minutes into the conversation I realized she wasn't the same Astra who'd left Dead End. She went on and on about parties she'd been to and people she'd met. I even heard a male voice in the background. She would barely even let me get a word in about anything going on in Dead End.

"Then she asked me to come visit and get to know Mamma. I know it sounds silly, but I felt betrayed. When Mamma abandoned us, it was Astra and I against the world. I told her I didn't need to go to Nashville to get to know my family. All the people who really loved me were in Dead End. She told me I was being childish, and that I had a mother who wanted to get to know me if I'd just give her a chance. I told her of course she'd side with the woman who abandoned us since she'd done the same thing as Mamma and abandoned me."

"Ouch."

"And my last words to her were, 'I'll never forgive you.' I didn't get a chance to talk to her before she hit the road with Jessi-Lyn. That day. I tried, but she told me she wasn't ready. She needed a night out with Jessi-Lyn first, then she'd be ready to talk. But I never got that chance.

"Then my entire world was turned upside down. With not only her death, but suddenly finding out I had a niece. I was so blown away by that knowledge. Another thing she'd kept from me, and I was grieving, overwhelmed with having a baby in the house and hating the world."

We sat in silence for a few moments, then Zeke said, "But then you adjusted. You've done a fantastic job with Teeny. She's a great kid."

"Yeah, she is, but I figure that's despite my influence, not because of it. I don't know what I'm doing half the time."

He chuckled. "I'll let you in a little secret. That's called being a parent. None of us knows what we're doing. We just figure it out as we go along and hope that one day we really do know as much as we pretend to."

"Yeah, I feel Astra would ace parenting as she did everything else. You don't know how many times I wish I could just take Teeny to the graveyard and tell Astra, 'Here. You fix this.'"

He nodded. "She was always good with people. Didn't matter if they were young, old, cranky, or stubborn. She always left them better than she found them. That summer we both worked at Jerry's I got a close-up view of it."

Jerry Don's Burger Barn. The last place I ever saw her

alive. Tears threatened to spill over my lids again, so I changed the subject. I pointed to the schedule on his desk. "Let Frank work behind the bar. He's terrible at it now, but he learns fast. I think if you spend just a couple of hours with him on a slow day and give him some pointers, he'll be ok. Matt has a history with Jenna, not Tammy. Put Jenna on front of the house the days she's working with Matt, and they won't run into each other as much. Oh, and Sinead dropped out of college and has been asking for more hours, so you can use her to fill in."

He scribbled all that down. "Boone should've left you in charge instead of me."

"No, my cousin knew exactly what he was doing when he left the bar in your hands." I just wish we knew what Boone was off doing. I had a feeling Granny knew. There wasn't a thing that went on in her family that she didn't know about. I wanted to talk to her about the visions.

Zeke was absorbed in remaking the schedule, so I patted him on the shoulder and said my goodbyes.

I found Granny upstairs in her usual spot in between customers. Aunt Tatty was lounging on the sofa. "Hey, Aunt Tatty, are you feeling, okay?"

"Why? Do I look sick?"

"Oh, no, you look fine to me. It's just Gayla is swamped down there and..." I didn't want to say what I was thinking. I loved Aunt Tatty. I just didn't like her all that much. I didn't like the way she treated Granny. I didn't like her waltzing downstairs to help whenever the mood struck her. It was none of my business if she didn't want to work there at all. She was well beyond retirement age, but it wasn't fair for her to have one foot on either side. She either helped out or she stayed out of our way.

"She'll figure it out. It'll build character." Aunt Tatty said.

Granny rolled her eyes. "Tatiana, get your lazy butt down there and help the girl! Besides, you're driving me crazy over there with your loud sighs."

"You won't let me touch the money. What am I supposed to do down there?"

"Crowd control," said Granny. "Now, go!"

"I tell ya, one of these days I'm gonna go get my own place, and then you're gonna miss me," Tatty said.

"You've been saying that for centuries, yet here you are still being a perpetual pain in my butt."

I grinned at Granny's exaggeration and Aunt Tatty's subsequent dirty look. I had a feeling Aunt Tatty would've stomped down the stairs if she didn't have arthritis in her knees. As it was, she slapped the magazine down on the coffee table.

"That woman is gonna drive me to homicide one of these days," Granny said. "Now, sit down here sweetie, and talk to me. What is it you're worried about?"

She continued shuffling the tarot cards. I swear if someone ever made a recording of that and put it in one of those white noise sleep apps, it would knock me out in minutes. It was one of the sounds of my childhood that made me feel both safe and content. I had to block it out now so I could stay on task.

"Why do you think I'm worried?" I'd purposely kept my tone light.

"I don't think. I know. Now come on, spill your tea."

I smiled. "It's spill *the* tea Granny."

She grabbed a notebook from beside her chair and wrote that down. She was forever collecting phrases that she hadn't heard before. Once when Holly had told her she was "on fleek" Granny insisted the only things she was on were fiber for regularity, and iron pills.

"So, spill it then. What's up?"

"One of the ghosts touched me." I waited for her reaction. But she continued to shuffle the cards. "And I saw her death and now I'm having spontaneous visions."

If that didn't get a reaction out of her, I wasn't sure what would.

She spread out three cards. The Nine of Pentacles reversed, the Five of Cups, and The Tower. "You're working too hard."

I sighed. "Granny, we've talked about this. I enjoy staying busy."

"No, you're working too hard to figure out your

visions." She pointed to the reversed Nine of Pentacles. Then she tapped the Five of Cups. "Allow yourself to grieve the past, then let it go."

"And you don't have to tell me what The Tower says. I can see the card. People are jumping out of a burning building. Disaster awaits."

Granny laughed. "The Tower is one of my favorite cards. I remember when you used to sit over there with your wooden blocks and build towers. You painstakingly arranged them so that you could go higher and higher. You said, 'Granny, I'm gonna build a tower as tall as the ceiling.' And you tried but you couldn't fight gravity and every time you got to a certain height, the whole thing would come tumbling down. But then you took your blocks and tried a new way. You built a bigger base. Once I found you trying to glue those blocks together. But I told you that was cheating."

"I don't remember any of this, Granny," I said.

She smiled. "You never gave up. You kept trying. And then one day you took your blocks into my bedroom over there and after a few minutes you came running out smiling. 'Granny, I did it! I built a tower as tall as the ceiling! Come see!' And I followed you into the bedroom and found all the blocks on the floor. At first, I thought they'd fallen down again, but then I saw they were in a pattern, stacked one after the other. 'See, Granny. It's as tall as the ceiling.' And by golly it was. It was just a horizontal tower instead of a vertical one."

She looked at me then. "There's more than one way to look at things, sweetie. You just have to change your perspective."

chapter
twenty-one

ON MONDAY MORNING, the gym was filled with people, both dead and alive. It was easy to tell the difference because the living held candles waiting to be lit. We'd all driven to the school together in Aunt Mer's Suburban but had split up as soon as we walked through the doors. Teeny found Kira and some of their friends. Aunt Mer had been accosted by a customer who had a question about hydrangeas, and that left me standing awkwardly by myself looking for a place to sit.

I took the steps up to the bleachers and almost took a spot in the first row where I always sat for Teeny's volleyball games, then I thought about what Granny said about changing my perspective. I knew she didn't mean my actual view of the gym or any given area, but I went with my gut and went to the top of the bleachers for a different view.

As soon as I sat, I scanned the crowd and found Carly at the bottom waving at me. I waved back, and she motioned me to come down and sit with her. I shook my head and indicated I wanted her up there with me. She shook her head and made her way up to me. "You had to pick the place furthest away?"

"I can see more up here."

She shoulder-bumped me. "See what? Dandruff in the hair of all the people sitting below you? We're so high up Grey's gonna look like an action figure."

"How's Grey doing?" I nodded to where he stood on the basketball court talking to a few other school officials.

"About the same." She shrugged.

The lights dimmed, and music began to play. Grey welcomed everyone, then had someone give the prayer. Then Coach Abbott stepped up to the microphone in the middle of the court. Coach Jake Abbott had to be close to retirement age. He'd been Astra's softball coach years ago, as well as her track and basketball coach. Teeny hadn't followed in her mamma's athletic footsteps. She only tried out for the volleyball team because Kira had. After he spoke, other coaches, and teachers, along with several students, paid their respects to Nessa. I couldn't tell you what any of them said because I was too focused on changing my perspective. What was it up here I was supposed to see?

Grey's voice brought my attention back to the middle

of the floor. "Thank you all for coming. Before we all part for today and go our separate ways. I want to honor Coach Anderson with a song, and I'd like us all to sing it together. He nodded to the band who'd been sitting in the bottom left section of the bleachers. And as the band director raised her baton, the first notes of the school fight song burst forth from the collective instruments. The mood of the crowd lifted almost instantly. Most of the folks here were either current or past Dead End students and, like me, probably remembered the many pep rallies where we ended with this song. Carly and I turned simultaneously and smiled at one another. I could almost see her braces and choker necklace as if she still wore them. We began to sing:

Dead End Spirits go big blue. Strong and mighty, always true. Vic-tor-y will not elude...

I spotted Rowdy heading along the east wall of the gym toward the coaches' offices. He was out of uniform, but I recognized his cowboy hat. He was wearing the same clothes he'd worn the night of his date with Holly. I continued to mouth the words of the song but kept my eyes on him. And as soon as we did the final battle cry and raised our fists in the air while chanting the letters D-E-H-S I shot down the steps with only a brief, "I'll catch up to you later," over my shoulder and wound my way through the crowd keeping my eye on Rowdy the whole time. He made his way across the gym floor, sticking close to the wall, and then I lost him for a bit because I got stuck behind slow moving tall people. Once they moved out of the way, I searched the crowd again near the same spot where I'd last seen Rowdy. I wanted to see if I could talk to him and trigger another vision.

I finally spotted him again right as he slipped into the coaches' office. What in the world was he doing in there? I bumped into Aunt Mer near the doors of the locker rooms talking to Sadie about ordering fall mums for the front office. I tried to step around them and continue toward the office, but Sadie flicked a glance at me and laid a hand on my arm. "Who on earth could imagine when I sent you and Jessi-Lyn out here the other day, that we'd all be meeting here to mourn Nessa's passing? It's a tragedy."

I saw Coach Abbott's face before me. *He sat at his desk, smiling. "That girl was a walking ray of sunshine if I ever saw one. She could illuminate a whole room with her presence. And she was a Braves fan like me. We'd spend hours talking about the latest game, recalling each home run and strike. Everyone around here is either an Astros or a Rangers fan. Not Astra. She recognized greatness when she saw it."*

I rolled my eyes.

"Nessa, don't tell me you're a Rangers fan or an Astros fan too."

"Hell no, the cubs are the best team that ever lived."

Then everything shifted, and he was looking sternly at

me. "You stay away from the Kendalls if you know what's good for you."

"You okay, hon?" Aunt Mer asked.

I shook my head as if to clear the vision. Sadie was also staring, and I realized I'd missed whatever she had asked me.

"I'll catch up with you later." I nodded to Sadie and dashed toward the office.

I stopped when I got near the door. What the actual hell was that? Coach Abbott talking about my sister. She loved the Braves. But where had that vision come from? Astra didn't have anything to do with this. And there was no ghost nearby. I leaned against the wall for support. I willed my heart to stop racing. I had to find out what Rowdy was doing in that office. I knew there was a back way in from the locker room area. But he came out while I was making my way around, then I'd miss him.

"What are you doing?"

I jumped and whirled around to find Carly behind me.

"Nothing."

"You shot off down the stairs and now you look like you're considering breaking and entering."

"It's not breaking and entering if someone else has already entered." I turned back toward the door.

"It doesn't work that way. But what are you talking about? Who is in there?"

When I didn't immediately answer, she took my arm and spun me around to face her. "Star! No. Stop it. You've got to drop your paranoia about Rowdy."

"It's not paranoia."

Just then, Mayor Abbott exited the office. What was he doing in there?

I didn't have a chance to voice those thoughts because the door opened again, and Rowdy stepped out and headed in the opposite direction.

I didn't even have to say a word. All I did was make eye contact with Carly.

She slowly shook her head. "That proves nothing. There is an explanation for this. Let me do some checking and I'll get back to you. But in the meantime, stand down. If there is something going on—and I'm not saying there is—you could be in danger. So, wait until you hear from me, got it?"

chapter
twenty-two

WHILE I HAD every intention of keeping my promise to Carly—probably—I was glad when she called early the next morning.

"I may have found something that supports your theory that Rowdy is involved."

"Okay?" I tried to keep my voice level, but my heart was pumping out of my chest.

"I've been going through traffic camera footage on the sly, searching Jessi-Lyn's neighborhood for anything suspicious, and Rowdy's truck entered the neighborhood at nine pm and didn't exit or at least not that I found before I had to get back on patrol."

"You saw him go into Jessi-Lyn's house?"

"No, there are no cameras near her house. But I can't imagine what he would've been doing in that neighborhood on that particular night. He lives on the other side of town."

"Did any of the neighbors mention seeing a truck that didn't belong when y'all canvassed the neighborhood that first day?"

"We only talked to the folks on her street and the ones directly in front and behind to see if anyone saw any suspicious activity at her house. But that big truck of his doesn't blend in. And he wouldn't have been dumb enough to park in front of her house. A smart criminal would've parked a couple of streets over and walked. I need to find out if anyone has seen it in the neighborhood recently, but specifically that night. But I can't go canvass the other streets now that the case is closed. It would get back to the department. And that's where you come in."

"Me? I told you what happened when I tried to talk to Rowdy at the dance. I failed miserably."

"Yeah, but that's because you were trying to question him. You need to go about it differently. Don't ask people questions. Get them to talk to you about themselves. Do what you do in your jobs at the Merc and the pub. Have organic conversations instead of reading questions off a list."

"I didn't read from a list," I insisted.

"No, but I know you. When you're trying to get information, you're as smooth as a pile of broken glass. Remember when you were trying to lie to Aunt Mer, that time when we were like twelve or something and wanted to go down to the lake alone and we came up with a great lie about how Uncle Paul was going to take us? You wrote it down and read it off to her."

I grinned. "Point taken, so what am I supposed to do, go knock on the doors and say, 'hey I'm Star, tell me about yourself and your life? And by the way, have you seen a big truck with running lights recently?' Like what even is my excuse for being there?"

She drummed her thumbs on the steering wheel for a few seconds, then whipped her head around. "I have the perfect idea!"

I put in a call to Aunt Willa Jo. "Hey, I have a free afternoon today. Can I come by and get your signs to start putting out today?"

"You sure, honey? You've had a rough few days and putting out signs is a lot of work. Give me a couple of days and let me see if I can line up someone else to help you later this week."

"I have someone. Carly is off today, and she's offered to help. We both just need a day of physical activity outdoors to get our minds off life, you know?" I tried to make my voice sound hopeless. It wasn't a stretch.

"Okay, honey. If you're sure. Come down to

campaign headquarters. I'll get Gavin to help load them up."

"Great! See you soon."

Carly and I drove out to the lavender farm. *Campaign headquarters* was a space in an old barn Uncle Gavin had cleaned out for Aunt Willa Jo. She ran the café on the farm and spent most of her time there anyway. We pulled up to the entrance of the barn and Uncle Gavin came out.

"Squirrely Davidson, as I live and breathe." Uncle Gavin held out his arms for a hug, and Carly let him envelop her. Uncle Gavin has called her Squirrely since we were kids because I got so excited when we met and I was trying to tell him about it after school and apparently, I was talking fast and my, "this girl Carly Davidson..." sounded like "Squirrely Davidson" and the name stuck.

"Hey, Gavin," Carly said.

"When are you going to run for Sheriff?" He winked at her.

"When you and Merilee quit pretending y'all aren't meant for each other." She winked right back and left him standing there with his mouth open as we walked over to where the signs were.

They were propped up in rows against the metal warehouse wall. Two by three-foot cardboard signs reading Willa Jo Bell for Mayor were sandwiched around a wooden stake which was flat on the top and pointed on the bottom for ease of sticking into the dirt. "I didn't know there were so many."

"Oh, this isn't even all of them. The bigger ones for the side of the road are out in the back." Aunt Willa Jo must have seen the fear in my face because she said, "Don't worry, sweetie, those aren't for you. We're getting a group together next week to help put them out. The ones you're taking are just for the people who've ordered one for their yard."

"And if you see a street where there's only one or two, and you really want to, you can knock on some doors and see if it's okay to put more out," Willa Jo said from behind me. She handed me a stapled stack of papers. "Thanks again, honey. Here are the names and addresses. Start wherever you want and only do what you want today. Don't feel obligated."

"I don't, okay. I really want to do this. I promise." I took the papers from her and ignored the guilt I felt in keeping from her the real reason why I was so excited to help out today.

"Carly, honey, you're such a sweetie for helping us out." Aunt Willa-Jo embraced her. "You're coming to game night tonight, right?"

"Wouldn't miss it. Monthly game night with the Bells is a tradition that cannot be broken. I'll bring my usual. And this time I'll splurge for the Double Stuffed." Carly winked.

It was a well-known fact in my family that Carly in the kitchen was a disaster. She was a competent cop, and an even better gamer, but packaged cookies were about the best she could do in contributing to the best part of game night—the food.

"That reminds me. I need to give Holly a call and remind her to put extra garlic butter on at least a half tray of the garlic cheese biscuits." Uncle Gavin said.

Aunt Willa Jo put her hands on her hips. "Thanks for the warning. I'll know not to play at your table tonight. The last time you nearly killed me with the garlic breath."

"Same for me," I chimed in.

Uncle Gavin nodded. "Now that's settled, and we know I'll be playing solitaire, let's get these girls loaded up so they can be on their way."

When we were on our way, I flipped through the list. "Looks like there are several signs ordered on Belladonna Lane. But Moonlight Drive only has two."

They were to the south of Jessi-Lyn. And yes, if you're wondering, they hadn't escaped the Great Renaming. They were formerly known as Oak and Pine Streets.

"Let's start there," Carly said. "We'll start on the corner and work our way down."

Carly stood in the yard with the sign as I knocked on the door. I ran through our cover story in my head. An elderly woman opened the door. "Hello?"

"Hi there, I'm with the Willa Jo Bell for mayor

campaign and I'm putting out some signs your neighbors ordered and wondered if you'd like one as well?"

"Willy who?" She hollered. "Aren't you a little young to be running for mayor?"

I wondered how old she was if she thought almost forty was young. "No, ma'am. I'm not the one running. And it's Willa Jo Bell. She owns the café out at Bright Lavender Farms."

She made a face. "I know her. She's one of Addie Bell's girls, isn't she? She doesn't go to my church. The mayor does though."

I wasn't sure if she was talking about Granny or Aunt Willa Jo or what church membership had to do with one's duties as a mayor. "Willa Jo Bell has been a city council member for the past—"

"So, this Willa Jo, is she is uppity as her Mamma? Is that why she's hired out someone to do her canvassing for her?

"No ma'am, she's my aunt and I'm just helping her out by delivering the signs people have ordered and—"

"Ordered? You want me to *pay* for one of those signs? I'm voting for Hank Kendall 'cause he's done a decent job. Better than that last guy who let them open a liquor store not four blocks from my church. But if I was gonna have a sign in my yard y'all should be paying me to advertise for you."

She began pulling the door closed.

"Hold on a moment, ma'am. Can I ask you one more thing? Then I'll go, I promise."

She stopped and gave me a look that meant, "this better be good."

Carly had come up with this, so I hoped it worked. "We're trying to get an idea of the issues residents are facing. For instance, a couple of your neighbors mentioned strange vehicles parking along the street. Have you noticed anything like that? Or any other issues?"

She let go of the door. "I certainly have! Arnie Sullivan in that yellow house down there, he parks his old Winnebago on the street and lets his wife's brother stay in it when he's trying to sober up."

I wrote that down on my clipboard. I had considered just pretending to write, but I was sure she'd notice. "Any others?"

"No, but there's often an odor in my backyard that smells like dirty feet and," she opened the door wider and pointed a finger over my shoulder, "the city hasn't trimmed the branches near the stop sign in ages, and I'm afraid it's gonna cover it up completely. Oh, and downtown there's a building that's been closed forever and no one is washing the windows, and they just look terrible. "And..."

She kept going, and I wrote everything down. When she'd exhausted her complaints and possibly herself, I said,

"Thank you for your feedback. I'll be sure to pass all this along to my aunt."

I tried not to be disappointed that she'd been no help identifying Rowdy's truck.

"Thank you for listening and for writing it all down, dear. And you know, I'm really gonna consider both candidates before I vote. I was going for Kendall because he's the devil I know. But if your aunt is as attentive as you are, then she might get my vote after all. I'm still not paying for a flimsy piece of cardboard in my yard, though." She shut the door in my face, and I held my laughter until I got out of sight.

I hit a few more houses—all of which were voting for Mayor Kendall—then reported back to Carly, who was waiting in the truck down the street. I grabbed a bottle of water from the small ice chest and said, "This is harder than I thought."

"Why do you think I'm in such good shape? I spend most of my day walking the streets of downtown." She slapped a thigh muscle. "You can't get quads like these without working them regularly."

"No, I mean talking to people."

Carly laughed and said, "Once you rest up, we have a few more houses on this side, then we can go over to the next.

. . .

Other folks, while less disparaging toward the Bells than the lady in the first house, were no help concerning Rowdy's truck. I was beginning to feel hopeless myself. We got donations for and placed six more signs, however, so it wasn't a total loss. And I wrote down all their complaints. We spent a few hours between the streets directly surrounding Jessi-Lyn's and moved to the last street in the neighborhood around supper time. We'd long since run out of signs but had placed many new orders and I was continuing to collect the complaints for Aunt Willa Jo. It's funny what people will complain about when you let them talk. One lady even suggested we change the name of Dead End into something cheerier, because it sounded so hopeless.

I walked up a sidewalk littered with various children's toys and told myself whatever came from this one; I was done for the day. I knocked on the door and a woman not much younger than me came to it with a baby on one hip and a toddler clinging to her legs. What sounded like cartoons blared from the tv and the smells coming from the baby made me queasy. I gave her my speech, and she refused a sign because—in her words—her husband didn't believe in the government. I asked about the issues, mentioning, as I had with each other house, strange vehicles parked along the street.

"Yeah, actually, there was one that parked right behind Bill's work truck the other night. One of those big ones with lights on the roof. It wouldn't normally be a problem, but he was on call and had to go out about eleven. We both usually park on the street because the kids like to play in the driveway. We don't have much of a backyard here. Anyway, the guy parked so close, Bill couldn't get out, so I had to get up and move my car so he could leave."

"Where exactly was it?"

"Right there where you're parked." She nodded to Carly's truck.

"Do you happen to have a doorbell cam?" I hadn't seen one, but the newer ones could look like anything.

"No, Bill doesn't like those. He won't even let me have an Alexis. He says he doesn't need the government spying on him in his own home."

I was about to ask what an Alexis was when I realized she was talking about that popular virtual assistant. I didn't bother to correct her on the name nor argue with her on her tinfoil hat theories.

"But Holly, over there. She has one. I know because once we had a package stolen off the porch and she helped us find who did it because her doorbell cam caught everything. I thought if anything, that would convince Bill we needed one, but he still said no."

I turned to where she was pointing and if I didn't have my hands full with the clipboard, I probably would've slapped myself upside the head for being so dense. It was Holly's house. *My* Holly. I'd been so exhausted I hadn't realized we were on her street. This was absolutely perfect! We didn't have to come up with any sort of story to get her doorbell cam footage. I thanked the woman and all but skipped back to the truck. I relayed our good news to Carly.

"Well, let's go talk to her!" she said. "So we can get the footage."

I glanced at the time on my lock screen on my phone. "She'll be headed to game night; we can talk to her there."

chapter
twenty-three

ON THE SECOND Tuesday of every month, Pub Dead closes early for a private event. That event being Bell Family—and Friends—Game Night. We took our gaming seriously. And everyone showed up. Even Granny and Aunt Tatty came downstairs for it.

It was a tradition Astra started when we were in high school. She loved party type games like *Cranium* and *Whoonu*. Granny loved *Skip-Bo*, and other card games, and Uncle Gavin and Uncle Buddy insisted on matching wits—or useless knowledge—with *Trivial Pursuit*, so to keep the peace, we usually had a few tables going and everyone could choose what they wanted to play.

I was hoping Holly would get there early so I could talk to her about Rowdy, but we were already seated and setting up the games when she arrived, and she joined in at the Skip-Bo table all the way across the room from where

Teeny, Kira, and I were sandwiched in between Aunt Willa Jo and Aunt Mer in a cutthroat game of *Nerts*. It's a card game kind of like multiplayer solitaire we'd played in our family for as long as I could remember.

My aunts took this game seriously. More people in the family used to play, but as the years went on, people got tired of getting accidentally sliced with a fingernail as hands flew placing cards in the middle of the table, or getting lashed by a sharp tongue when things weren't going well for one of the aunts. I loved it too, but mostly played to make sure Aunt Mer and Aunt Willa Jo didn't choke each other across the table.

My Aunts loved each other and got along great when not playing Nerts, but there was something about it that brought out the inner demon in both of them.

"Will, I swear on our mother's very own soul, I'm gonna upturn this table if you don't quit forgetting to turn your stack over when you complete it," Aunt Mer said.

"I don't have time to do that. I have cards to play. And besides, it's not a rule," Aunt Willa Jo replied.

Aunt Mer shot back, "Fine, then I'm throwing out your asinine rule of not being able to play with two hands. God wouldn't have given me two hands and if he didn't mean for me to use them."

Aunt Mer threw out an ace of diamonds with her left hand, while her right placed a king of spades on top of a queen and turned over the deck, indicating that the stack was complete.

"Merilee, I'm gonna break your fingers. One. Hand."

"I'm gonna stab both of you if you don't keep these stacks straight," grumbled Kira. "The diamonds are over here in the hearts, and I can't see what card I can play."

Teeny shot me an anxious look. I had only one card left in my Nerts pile and—there! I slammed the ten of clubs down on the nine ending the round and hollered, "Nerts!"

Both aunts gave incredulous cries, and Kira laid her head on the table. "I had ten cards left in my Nerts pile."

They each told me their scores and I recorded them carefully on the notepad, then glanced back at Zeke, who was still alone. "Hey, y'all continue without me. I'm gonna play with Zeke. He's all alone over there."

"I'll come too," Teeny jumped up from her chair and was halfway to Zeke before anyone could react.

Kira snatched the score pad and said, "Sweet! With you two gone, that puts me in second place."

"You keep these two banshees in line, you hear?" I said to Kira over my shoulder and crossed the room to Zeke's table. As soon as I got there, I realized I'd left one hell and slid into another. It was one of the weird strategy games he and Boone usually played. It had more pieces than all the other games combined. But his face lit up when he saw me, so I couldn't back down.

"Pick a color."

Teeny slid into a chair and took black.

"What game is this?" I sorted through the small plastic bags of game pieces he gave me and chose my favorite color, turquoise.

"*Five Tribes*. You're gonna love it," Grey said behind me.

"Perfect. Now we have four players." Zeke rubbed his hands together. "Grey, you want orange or pink?"

Grey picked up the small plastic bag containing pink game pieces and said, "I'm a confident male. Nothing wrong with pink."

Zeke nodded and took the orange pieces for himself.

I scanned the room and then turned back to Grey. "Where's Carly?"

"She was called into work. Again."

That left it up to me to talk to Holly about her doorbell cam. After the game. But that ended up being much later. *Five Tribes* turned out to more fun than I first thought, but the rules themselves took about a half hour, and the gameplay itself took longer that. By the time we finished most everyone else had packed up their things and were mingling by the door. I searched for Holly and found her stacking chairs on the tables.

"Teeny, can you help Zeke put up the game? I need to go talk to Holly."

She nodded.

I reached Holly and lifted the last chair around a four top. "We have a break in the case."

She blinked a few times. "A break in what case?"

"Nessa's murder."

"But that was ruled an accident. And who is we, Star?"

"Carly. She found video of Rowdy's truck in Jessi-Lyn's neighborhood on the night of the murder, and we went door to door in the neighborhood and turns out he was parked not too far from your house. Your neighbor said you had a doorbell cam, so we just need to look at the footage and—"

"Stop." Holly sat on a bar stool and patted the one beside her, indicating I should join her. "Rowdy didn't kill Nessa."

"Yes. He did. I know it wasn't an accident." I explained about Caroline and the visions I'd been having. "If you would just look at your doorbell cam footage you'll see."

"But Star—."

"Also, Jessi-Lyn said she caught Nessa and him together at a seedy bar," I finished.

"Did Nessa tell you why she was there with him?"

"No, she doesn't remember anything past Labor Day."

She nodded. "Because I do. He told me everything. He's not the one you're looking for."

I remembered the night Carly and I were at Karaoke. "You can't know that."

Holly opened her mouth to speak, but I held up my hand. "Hold on, let me finish. You spent twenty minutes with him at a bar and you said he spent most of that time on the phone texting Nessa."

"Are you done now?" Holly asked.

I let out a breath. "Yeah."

"You remember I left the bar that night because my date with him was a bust?"

"Yeah."

"He left not soon after I did, and I ran into him in the parking lot after I dropped my phone and it slid under my car. He crawled under and got it for me, and I don't know, a switch just flipped and before I knew it, we were making out in my car."

"Oh hell. You had car sex in a public parking lot with a murderer. You coulda died, Holly."

"Stop it! Let me finish. No, we didn't have sex in the car. I stopped it there."

"Good!"

She lowered her voice. "But I had him follow me home. My doorbell cam will show us walking up to my front door and practically undressing each other on my front porch. He didn't kill Nessa. He was with me."

I let that sink in for a moment. "Maybe he snuck out when you fell asleep?"

"I didn't fall asleep. We were awake until at least three."

"You always say you're awake when we're watching old home movies too, but your snores say different."

"I was awake. I was very much awake. Several times. All. Night. Long." She waggled her eyebrows to drive the point home.

"Ewww! I don't need details."

"Apparently you did. Anyway. After we finished... *being awake*, I sent him on his way and went into work. Detective Palmer said Jessi-Lyn found Nessa shortly after midnight. Rowdy never left my bed until well after that."

I let all that sink in. "But he was texting Nessa while he was supposed to be on a date with you that first night. Did you ask him about that?"

"I didn't. Not that night. But we've talked about it since then and it's...complicated. And don't look at me like that. It's not the same kind of *complicated* you're thinking of. Ask him yourself. He's here to pick me up."

Rowdy didn't seem happy to see me with Holly, but once she explained what was going on, the muscles in his jaws relaxed, but he kept a tight grip on the steering wheel.

"So that's why you were upset at the dance?" he asked. "You thought I murdered Nessa?"

"She had a vision, and you were in it. I told you how

we all have unique abilities? You saw mine the other night." She grinned in a way that made me not want to know any more. "Star's is talking to the dead, and more recently, seeing their deaths as if it's happening to her."

"You saw who killed Nessa?" The look on his face wasn't guilt or fear of being caught. It was something else. Hope?

"No, it doesn't quite work like that. But can you explain why you and your dad were in Nessa's office together at the memorial?" I asked.

"I was in my uncle's office and my dad followed me in and we had words. We don't care much for each other."

"Your uncle's office? Coach Abbott is your uncle?"

"Well, by marriage. Ex-uncle. He was married to my Aunt Sadie."

"I'd forgotten that." They'd been divorced for years. Probably about as long as Zeke and Jessi-Lyn.

"I can't believe you thought I was capable of murder. You've known me most of my life, Star."

"Not really. I knew the boy you were, but you've been gone for years. And there were all kinds of rumors about why you left. Why did you?"

He massaged the back of his neck. "It's complicated."

"That word keeps popping up where you're concerned," I said.

"Yeah, well, we Kendalls are."

"About that..." I told him about the vision I had there

at the memorial with Coach Abbott warning Nessa to stay away from the Kendalls. "Why would he do that?"

"Beats me." He shrugged. "Listen, how about you back off and let those who know what they're doing handle it? You're treading dangerous waters, here. You feel me?"

I stared at him a beat, then said. "I feel you."

I felt a chill run down my spine is what I felt. He was still lying to me. He had nothing to do with Nessa's death, but he either knew who did, or had a pretty good idea.

chapter
twenty-four

I **WAS ITCHING** to discuss things with Carly, but because of her late shift, I knew she'd be sleeping in. Instead, I spent the morning refereeing Granny and Aunt Tatty at the Merc. When it was an appropriate time to call Carly, I took my break and went out to the back alley to get some peace.

"Rowdy's not our guy."

"Yeah, I know. I got my ass chewed out by Sheriff Briggs." She only called him that when she was mad at him or on the job. Otherwise he was Uncle Paul.

"Seriously? What happened?

"He called me into his office at the end of my shift this morning and said my login had been recorded accessing traffic cams, but he wasn't aware of any cases I was working on where'd I'd need to do that. So, I told him I hadn't wanted to accuse a fellow officer until I had just cause. And told him about seeing Rowdy and the mayor at the gym. That's why I'd accessed the cams."

My stomach clenched. "What did he have to say about that?"

"He thanked me for letting him know and told Rowdy had an alibi for that night. And he left me with, 'Goddaughter or not, I swear to God I will suspend your ass if you ever do anything like this again.'"

"Ouch."

"Yeah, so we have to drop it, Star. I'm serious. I can't lose my job."

"He wouldn't really fire you, would he?"

"Oh, he would. He takes policy seriously."

"I'm sorry." I really was, but I wasn't going to drop it. I was, however, going to carry on without her. But that part, I was keeping to myself.

"Hey, I feel bad about missing game night last night. How about you, me, and Grey hang out tonight?" Carly suggested.

"*Supernatural, Buffy,* or *Gilmore Girls*?" I'd never watched *Supernatural* when it first aired, Grey had never watched *Buffy*, and Carly was a *Gilmore Girls* virgin, so we were taking turns watching/rewatching the three series together.

"*Buffy*, of course! Now that we've gotten through that first season, Grey is addicted. He's threated to watch it without us."

"I knew we'd get him hooked. It was totally the Halloween episode, wasn't it?"

"Probably," Carly sounded distracted. "Hey, getting another call. Gotta go. See you tonight!"

When I got back to the house a few hours later, supper was just going on the table, but to my surprise it wasn't Aunt Mer who'd cooked. Teeny and Kira stood among the sea of dirty dishes looking pleased. "We made meatloaf."

I smiled and hoped the mess they'd made correlated to the tastiness of the dish. "How was school?"

"Aunt Mer already grilled me on that. Here's the abridged version. It was school," Teeny said, hands on hips.

It had been their first day back, but I should've remembered the unspoken rule of not asking a teenager how their day at school was. "Where is Aunt Mer?"

"There was an emergency at the lavender farm." She held up her fingers and did air quotes when she said the word emergency. "Uncle Gavin came by and got her."

Emergency indeed.

Kira pulled the silverware out of the drawer, then looked at me. "Doesn't it feel weird that your aunt and uncle are sneaking around, borking everywhere?"

"Kira!" Teeny shoved her. "Hush! There will be no bork talk during dinner, especially old people bork talk."

Kira leaned down to pick up the forks Teeny had knocked out of her hand and said, "Fine, no bork talk, but what is their problem? Why can't they just come clean and bork like normal people?"

"Don't make me stab you with that fork, K. I'm serious." Teeny grabbed the utensils out of Kira's hand and tossed them in the sink, then retrieved new ones from the drawer.

Kira looked at me. "Am I too nosey? My mom says I am."

"Your mom is one to talk," I said. Then immediately regretted it. "Sorry."

Kira shrugged. "You don't have to tell me how annoying my mom is. Believe me. I live with it every day. But I wanna know something. If she was your sister's best friend, why didn't you two ever get along? I mean, even before..."

Before she drove Astra off the bridge? Is what she meant but left unsaid.

I pulled a chair out and sat. "It all goes back to Astra's slumber party in the eighth grade. Your mom brought a Ouija board and—"

"My mom? Jessi-Lyn Gibson? She had a Ouija board? Not possible."

"Yup, and she acted like she was an expert. She forced everyone outside to the front porch because, in her words, the light of the moon would help the spirits connect with us." I smirked at the memory.

"I would have left them to it, but she was moving the flange and telling people things like they'd never get a boyfriend, or their boobs would stay small, or someone they loved would die within the next five years. And everyone believed her. Except Astra, who knew she was full of crap but adored your mom anyway. I was about to say something, but there was a spirit in a rocking chair who followed your mom everywhere. She shook her head and said, 'I raised you better than that June Bug.'"

"June Bug? That's what Mamma called me when I was little." Kira scrunched her forehead.

I nodded and continued. "I made eye contact with the woman so she knew I could see her, and she said, 'Tell Jessi-Lyn her Memaw loves her but that she needs to straighten up and fly right.'

"So, I said, 'Hey, June Bug, straighten up and fly right.' Your mom dropped the flange and went as pale as the moon. She scrambled up and said, 'What did you say?'"

"I said, 'Your Memaw is ashamed of you.'"

I felt my cheeks warm with the memory. "I should've just given her the message, but I was tired of Jessi-Lyn bossing everyone around, especially Astra. So, I embell-ished and told her that Memaw watched her all the time and saw what she did behind closed doors and was ashamed of her, so she'd better start being nicer to people. She ran out into the yard and tripped over a tree root and that's when she broke her nose."

We sat in silence for a moment and then Teeny threw a glob of lumpy mashed potatoes across the table and they hit Kira in the middle of her forehead.

"What the heck, Teeny?" Kira scooped the mess off her forehead.

"I was just trying to break the awkward silence." Teeny shrugged.

A food fight ensued then, and I'm not ashamed to admit I fully participated in it. I was pulling bits of green peas out of my hair when the screen door slammed and Grey hollered, "Knock Knock!"

Kira stood with a spoon full of mashed potatoes in the corner of the kitchen, ready to ambush Grey as he walked in. I didn't even have time to warn him before the gooey white mess hit him right in the forehead. He stuck a finger in the potatoes and shoved it into his mouth and grinned. "No one told me we were having a food fight. I would've brought gravy. But as it is, all I have is some of Issacs Brain Matter Crunch."

Both of the girls sprinted toward him, and he gave them the half gallon. It was their favorite. It was Isaac's concoction which contained crushed Butterfinger candy bars, whole mini popcorn flavored jellybeans, and toasted pecans in a rich vanilla bean ice cream. They grabbed two spoons and ran giggling from the kitchen.

"Perhaps my peace offering worked?" He smiled.

"You didn't need to do that," I said.

"So, I guess I can just throw this one away?" He presented me with my own favorite. Zombie Nails. It was just a goofy name for Pistachio Almond. But it somehow tasted better.

"Not a chance. And thank you!" I took the other half gallon from him and got three bowls down from the cabinet.

"Oh, um, we only need two. Carly isn't coming," he said.

"Seriously? Again?" I sighed and put one of the bowls back. "Fine, but we're still watching *Buffy*!"

Twenty minutes into our second episode of the evening, Teeny decided we needed stove-top popcorn and asked me to make some. She claimed mine was better than hers, but I suspected it was because she was burritoed in her favorite blanket and didn't want to move.

While I was popping the corn, Kira came in and climbed up on the counter and searched through the top of the cabinets where Aunt Mer usually hid the candy. I was never sure why she hid candy when we had stuff like cokes, cereal, and other sugary foods within reach. Plus, we weren't five. My theory was she hid it, so she didn't have to share it with us.

She tossed me the bag of candy and began her descent. "Is it true you talked to Nessa?"

"I did. Did your mom tell you that?"

"No, Teeny did. Mom won't talk about it at all."

"Where is she tonight?" I asked Kira.

She shrugged. "At home. She said she needed a night of not dealing with anything."

I poured the popcorn into two bowls; one for the girls to share and one for Grey and me to share. Then added peanut M&M's to both.

"Can I talk to Nessa? Through you, I mean. I just want to tell her..." She turned away from me then. "I hate that she died thinking that voodoo doll was about her."

"She doesn't remember any of that, honey. She only remembers up until Labor Day, apparently. When she and your mom went on a camping trip or something."

"That's when they broke up. Or at least right after that. They were happy and going away for the holiday, and then they weren't."

"I'm sorry," I said. I truly was. Despite my feelings for Jessi-Lyn, I adored Kira. I'd watched her grow from a drooling baby to this amazing kid. I wanted to see her happy and well.

"But you know what that means? That was before they broke up, so she died with happy memories." She perked up and grabbed the sodas out of the fridge and balanced her bounty in her arms while I took the bowls, and we headed back to the living room.

Strike that. She wasn't an amazing kid. She was an amazing, well-adjusted young woman.

We settled back onto the sofa with Grey and Teeny and clicked play on the next *Buffy* episode. I don't even remember which one it was because my brain was stuck on something, and I couldn't quite place what it was. But it had been there since Kira mentioned Labor Day. That occasion kept coming up in different conversations. Jessi-Lyn didn't want to talk about it. Not just that. She completely clammed up when it was mentioned. As if she were scared of something. And the last vision of Nessa didn't make sense at all. The one where Coach Abbott was talking to her about Astra. Why would they be discussing my sister? That was it. That was what was caught in my brain brambles. If that was before Labor Day, she would remember. I needed to talk to Nessa again. I suppose I could ask Coach Abbott, but how do you go up to someone and say, "Hey, I saw in a vision that you were talking about my dead sister to your dead coworker. What's up with that?"

"I need some air. Be right back." What I needed was to talk to Caroline, but the reason why would take too long to explain. And everyone was too engrossed in evil Angelus, so no one followed me.

I found Caroline laying on the grass staring up at the stars. She sat up and smiled when she saw me.

"Hey, Star. What are you doing out here?"

I plopped down onto the blanket beside her, careful to keep a good distance. "I have a question. Do you remember the days right after your death?"

"Oh, I do. I couldn't quite figure out where I was at first, nor why no one could see me. I was at the hospital, you see. Where I was supposed to have my surgery. But until Doctor Levi told us about that the other day, I had no idea why I'd been there. But I was in several other places too. It was as if I kept...well...it didn't make a lick of sense then, but you know how your Uncle Gavin loves that space show with the guy who has the pointy ears. I can see it through the window when he and your Aunt Mer cuddle on the couch and watch it. Well, this pointy eared fella and his outer-space captain stand on a spot in the ship and then they say something to the ship and then it takes them there like magic?"

I smiled. "The Transporter."

"I can never hear what they say, since your Aunt Mer refuses to open the windows. But yes, it's like that. Except I didn't have to say a thing. Whatever place popped into my mind, that's where I went. I eventually learned to control it. And that's how I fetched the doctor the other day. I thought about him and there I was. Then I thought about you, and we were back again."

I told her about Nessa. "So, when she kept disappearing at Jessi-Lyn's, she was thinking about other places?"

"Possibly."

What places besides Jessi-Lyn's would Nessa think about? Her apartment, which was locked, and we'd never get into. The school was also locked because it was nighttime. But I knew someone who could get me in there. And it was worth a try.

Grey unlocked the doors, went in ahead of us, and flipped on the lights. It had been way too easy to convince him to bring me here. I told him that Kira wanted to talk to Nessa for closure. I could have told him the whole truth, but I didn't have time for that. And yes, I knew which buttons to push to get him to cooperate. Not proud of that at all. I scanned the immediate area for Nessa but didn't see her anywhere and told my companions as much.

We headed across the gym toward her office and right as Grey reached out to unlock the door, Nessa herself appeared.

"She's here." I didn't even have time to explain to her what I needed or even get into position before Nessa grabbed my arm and said, "My office. There's a body."

But that's all I heard before I was plunged into Nessa's death scene. Again, everything went dark. *I was at the bottom of the staircase in Jessi-Lyn's house. "You should've kept your nose out of it. She's dead and no one will ever find her." I recognized the voice, but I just couldn't place it. It was guttural, primal even. Someone who hated me or feared me. The only way I can describe it is like that game show when they play just a few notes of the music, and you have to guess what song and artist it was. You know the song, it's on the tip of your tongue.*

Then the gym reappeared again, and Grey was kneeling above me, cradling me in his arms. I blinked a couple of times, then sat up.

"I thought you were going to give us a warning, so I'd be ready to catch you," he accused.

"I didn't have time. Nessa touched me before I could open my mouth." I put my hands under me to push myself up.

"Why don't you sit here a minute before trying to get up," he said.

"I'm fine."

"Are you sure, Star?" A small voice croaked from behind me. I turned to find Teeny staring at me, pale-faced, and mouth set in a look that was so like her Mamma it hurt. She clung to Kira. I reached out to her, "I'm okay, honey."

She let go of Kira, threw her arms around me, and didn't let go or speak for a while. When she finally did, she whispered in my ear, "Don't ever do that again."

Once I stood up, and felt steady on my feet, I asked, "So what did it look like on y'all's end?"

Gray said, "You said 'There's Nessa,' then you went completely still as if you weren't there anymore. It wasn't you behind your eyes, Star. Then you swayed."

"Grey was like The Flash," Kira said. "He moved so fast and caught you just as you stiffened and fell backwards."

"I wouldn't say I was that quick." Grey grinned.

The words Nessa said to me came back in a rush. "Nessa said there was a body in her office."

Kira took a step toward the office. "A body? Who?"

Grey unlocked the door and swung it open. Nessa was nowhere in sight, but a pair of shoe clad feet stuck out from behind Nessa's desk.

twenty-five

GREY PULLED OUT HIS PHONE. "Get the girls and get out of here. Now. I don't want any of you involved in another crime scene. Go!"

I dashed to the girls. "Let's go."

I grabbed their hands and began pulling them along.

Kira tried to pull away from me, but I'd spent an entire summer scooping ice cream in Isaac's ice cream shop and had a grip. "Who is it?"

"I don't know, honey. But we can't help them now. Let's go!" It sounded cold, I knew it did, but once the police got here everyone here would be a suspect and I wasn't putting Teeny through that again, nor Kira.

We made it to my Jeep and out of the school parking lot just as the sirens wailed in the distance. Kira said from the back seat. "My mom won't answer her phone. What if that's her in there?"

"I'm sure she's okay, honey. There's no reason to think your mom would be in Nessa's office—this time of night, especially. Besides, you said she was staying in tonight, right?"

"Unless she thought Nessa was there and just wanted to be closer to her. Why won't she answer her phone?" She broke down then and sobbed against Teeny's shoulder in the back seat.

"Let's drive by your house so you can see that she's safe."

In a few moments, we pulled into their driveway and the house was not only dark but locked. I used hands-free to dial Zeke's direct number and when he answered, I said, "I'm about three minutes out, and I need you to meet me out front. I have Kira with me. She's not injured or anything, but she needs her dad right now."

He was waiting outside of Pub Dead when we drove up. Of course, there wasn't a single parking space, so I told Teeny to go with Kira and I'd park and be back as soon as I could. By the time I made it back, Teeny had texted that they were upstairs in Zeke's apartment.

As soon as I parked, I texted Grey, asking if the body was Jessi-Lyn. He hadn't answered yet. When I opened the door, Kira rushed toward me. "You said you only saw feet. What shoes did they have on?"

Zeke was giving me a "what the hell" look and promised with his eyes he'd be giving me an earful later about dragging his daughter along on my shenanigans. Okay, so maybe I read way more into that look than was there, but he was definitely not happy.

I thought back to what I had seen in the office. It had been such a quick glance. What shoes had I seen? They'd been blue. Light blue. They weren't heels, or any type of dress shoe. And then suddenly everything came into focus. "They were light blue Vans."

"Light blue? You're sure?" she asked.

I nodded. "Yeah, because I remember thinking how clean they were and how could anyone keep light blue shoes that clean."

"My mom has navy vans, but nothing light blue." Kira seemed to relax slightly, then tense again just as quickly. "Unless she bought them recently. And if they were clean, she might have. She does that a lot. Goes shopping when she's upset. Maybe she bought them today."

I checked my phone again. No word from Grey yet.

Zeke said, "Kira, baby, let's not make assumptions until we know more."

"But even if it's not her, someone else is dead. Someone at my school. I don't feel safe." She burst into tears again. "Maybe it's our fault."

She looked at Teeny and Teeny responded with, "Ours? How?"

"The voodoo doll. Maybe we opened some door we didn't mean to."

"What was this voodoo doll for anyway and why were y'all fighting about it?" Zeke asked. "I keep hearing about it, but no one will tell me anything about it."

The girls exchanged a look.

Zeke shook his head. "Nope. Don't even think about trying to sidestep this. I respect your privacy, but things are happening now that change that."

"I'm trying to find my dad," Teeny said in a small voice.

Of course, that's what the voodoo doll was about. I should've known.

Zeke's whole face changed. He lost the freaked-out parent look and kindness filled his eyes. "Your dad?"

Teeny nodded.

Kira said, "It's all my fault. Don't be upset with Teeny. I just...I think it sucks Teeny's mom died without ever telling anyone who her father is. Mom was talking one night about those days and how Teeny's mom was her best friend in the universe. So, I asked her if she knew and she said no, and she felt bad because she'd been so wrapped up in her own drama that she didn't even realize Astra had left town until she sent her a postcard from the road."

"I had no idea that Astra hadn't told Jessi-Lyn she was leaving," I said.

"She didn't tell any of us. At Jerry's I mean," Zeke said.

Kira continued, "Mom said when Astra came back,

she told her about Teeny and Mom asked who the father was and Astra's answer was, 'he was some mistake I made on the road.'"

I glanced at Teeny, and her face was scarlet. I opened my mouth to say something, but Zeke beat me to it. He lifted her chin and said, "You look at me. Your Mamma didn't mean that *you* were a mistake. She loved you. I know it."

Teeny turned her head to shrug away from his touch and he dropped his hand but didn't stop talking. "The Astra Bell I knew would never think her own child, no matter how she came into the world, was a mistake."

"I wouldn't know because she didn't stick around long enough to show me differently, but more importantly, what kind of guy was my dad that she wouldn't tell him he had a kid? That's why I didn't want Kira to make the doll."

"That's why y'all were fighting over it," I said.

They both nodded.

"You don't want to find your father?" Zeke asked.

"Would I like to know who my dad is? Yeah. I've seen so many photos of my mom, and I know I have her eyes, and her smile, but this nose? No one in the family has it."

It was a cute, upturned nose covered with freckles and one of my favorite things about her, but she was right. That nose was nowhere on our side of the family.

"But if he was someone my mom didn't want in her

life, then maybe I shouldn't be looking for him. Maybe I'm just inviting in trouble with an engraved invitation as Granny says."

"I'm sorry, Teeny. I didn't mean for any of this to happen." Kira grabbed her hand. "But when I found that part in the diary about NA. I knew it had to be him."

"NA?" Zeke asked.

"Yeah, Teeny and I found her mamma's old diary in the attic—that's what she crawled into my window to get that night—and I took it home with me one day without telling Teeny. I thought maybe I could find some clue in it. She never said anything about who Teeny's father was, but in this one entry she wrote, 'I have to tell NA about the baby.' There was a line over it, and she wrote in the margin. 'Nope. not gonna happen.' So, I figured out that NA was probably Teeny's dad. And I found a spell in one of the books at The Merc for help in finding missing objects. I tore out that page and put it in the pocket. Teeny was so mad." Tears streamed down Kira's face and Teeny wrapped her arms around her.

"It's okay," Teeny murmured.

"And so far, Teeny's dad hasn't shown up," Kira continued, "but there have been two people drop dead. So yeah, I think we did this."

I put a hand on her shoulder. "No, honey. That's not how magic works. You weren't trying to cause harm to anyone, you were only trying to find someone."

Teeny said, "I tried to get the doll back so I could destroy it, and but Coach found us fighting over it and confiscated it."

"That's what hurts most of all about this. Nessa died thinking I hated her. I didn't. I loved her." Tears filled Kira's eyes. "She made my mom so happy. And I liked having her around. I was hoping they'd get married, and I'd have a bonus mom, and now I might not have even one mom."

Zeke engulfed her in a hug, and she sobbed into his chest as he stroked her hair and Teeny rubbed her back. My phone dinged then, and a message from Grey popped up.

"You have a mom, honey. Grey just texted. It's not your mom in Nessa's office."

"You're sure?"

"I'm sure."

She burst into fresh tears. This time I imagined ones of relief.

A few minutes later, Jessi-Lyn herself called after having found over a dozen missed calls from Kira. She swung by to pick her up a bit later and assured her several times she was okay and real. Kira clung to her. The look on Jessi-Lyn's face almost made this scare worth it. I remembered her words about how she thought Kira hated her. Not that I wanted any of this to happen, nor did she I'm sure, but she had validation her daughter loved and needed her very much.

"Oh, Star, I have something for you." Jessi-Lyn reached into her purse and brought out my amulet. "You forgot it again the other day."

I took it from her hand. "Thank you."

My phone rang then. On the other end, Holly said, "Star, can you come over? I really need to talk."

"You okay?"

"Yeah. I just don't want to be alone right now."

"I'll be right there."

She thanked me and hung up.

Jessi-Lyn disentangled herself from Kira's grasp and said, "I'm headed out too. I have errands to run. You coming, K?"

"She's welcome to stay with me," Zeke said.

"No, I wanna go with Mamma." Kira kissed Zeke on the head. "I'll see you later, Daddy."

Jessi-Lyn beamed. "You sure, honey? I'm just going to be getting groceries and stuff."

"Yeah."

"Teeny, you can come too," Jessi-Lyn said.

Teeny looked to me and I nodded. "Keep your phone on."

They all headed out and Zeke said, "Star, can I talk to you about something?"

He had a serious look on his face, and I knew exactly what he wanted to talk about. He was pissed I'd taken Kira along with me to the school, and yeah, I'd be mad too if the tables were turned, but I didn't have any spoons left to deal with that and Holly sounded like she really needed to talk so I said, "Yeah. We're definitely gonna talk, but for now I need to go see what's up with Holly."

Holly's house was dark, but she answered the door seconds after I rang the doorbell and pulled me inside the house and locked the door behind her.

"Rowdy isn't answering my calls." She paced the foyer.

"I was at his place. He got a call. And he said it was about Nessa. Then he took his off-duty gun and put it in the waistband of his jeans. I asked him why he needed a gun and he said he hoped he wouldn't need it, but he didn't know who to trust anymore. I asked him who he was going to see, and he told me he'd tell me everything later. Then he took his truck key off his keychain, pocketed it, and handed me the keyring. He asked me to lock up for him and said he'd come by my place later. But that's been hours."

"Maybe he's been tied up in whatever this is and just hasn't had a chance to call?" I didn't believe it, but hoped it was true.

Her pacing increased. It was unnerving to see Holly

like this. She was a rock. But now she needed a rock, and I was going to be that for her. I took her hand. "Come into the kitchen."

She let me lead her in and I pointed to a chair at the table, then pulled out stuff to make us both a cup of tea.

Meanwhile, I texted Carly and told her to call me as soon as she was available. The phone rang almost immediately. "What's up?" Carly asked.

I explained the situation to her, and she was silent for a bit. Then said, "I'm on my way over."

A bit later, a knock sounded on the side door, and I let Carly in.

Holly looked up. Her face fell when she saw Carly. "Is he...is Rowdy dead?

"I don't know. But right now, we have another problem. Jake Abbott is dead—a gunshot wound to the chest —and Rowdy's name was written in blood on the floor next to him."

"Rowdy didn't kill his uncle," Holly said.

"I'm not saying he did, but there's a manhunt going on now for him. So, do you have any clue where he could be?"

"No, I don't."

Carly wrapped her arms around Holly from behind. "I'm sorry. I had to ask. It's my job. Even when it's not pleasant, it's still my job to ask the tough questions."

"I know," Holly said. "That's why I quit the law office

and opened Mourning Brew. There's nothing hard about breakfast."

"Look, I know Rowdy. He's a good cop. And while good cops have been known to go bad, I'm not sure that's what's happened here. If you hear from him at all, just let me know. I just want to talk to him."

Holly nodded.

"I've gotta get home," I said. "But I don't want to leave you alone, so how about you pack your pjs and we can have a cousin's slumber party like old times."

Holly stood. "No, I'm gonna stay here. In case Rowdy comes back. I'll be fine. I promise. Besides, I know you still have the same bed you had as a teenager. That thing wasn't the most comfortable bed back then, and since I have to get up at the ass crack of dawn, as you say, I need a good night's sleep."

Carly motioned to me. "Can you follow me out?"

I did as she asked and as soon as we got to the front porch she said, "What the hell, Star? You convinced Grey to break into the school? After I told you to stay out of it?"

"We didn't break in, Carly. He's the principal." I planted my hands on my hips. "And maybe if you'd been there like you said you'd be, then you could've stopped us."

She whipped around to face me. "Don't you think I would've been there if I could've? There is no other place I would've rather been tonight than with my two best friends, snuggled on the couch watching Buffy kick some vampire ass, but Rowdy didn't show up to work and I was called in. Then all hell broke loose when the call came in. And you better believe the sheriff is going to grill me about why you and Grey were there. I'm walking a thin line here, Star, and you're not making it any easier."

I wanted to defend myself, and to argue more, but one look at her glassy eyes and I drew her in and wrapped my arms around her.

"I'm sorry," I whispered.

She pulled away from me. "Me too. But sorry won't help anything right now."

chapter
twenty-six

HOLLY MIGHT HAVE HATED my bed, but to me it
so was heavenly that I overslept again the next morning
and didn't get to The Merc until fifteen minutes after I
should've been there. I'd called her on the way to see if
there'd been any word from Rowdy—there hadn't—and
she sounded like she hadn't slept at all. Aunt Tatty had a
line at least twelve people deep. And she was once again
trying to handwrite each ticket. I slid in beside her and
said, "I've got this."

A few minutes later, Teeny came back with two iced
coffees and began bagging the customer's purchases. The
school was closed again because the gym was a crime
scene, and I hadn't wanted to leave her at the house alone.
Thankfully, she didn't want to be there either. The store
was mostly empty except for a customer toward the front
Aunt Tatty was trying to upsell a crystal ball to.

I was straightening the candle wall when Palmer walked through the door of The Merc. He raised his eyebrows as he looked around and seemed to be searching for someone. Me, probably, but I wasn't planning on making it easy for him. I stayed crouched down, organizing the tapers. The phone rang then but thankfully Teeny answered it, then she hollered to me, "Star! Phone!"

I popped up then, and Detective Palmer stepped toward me and said, "Could I have a moment of your time, Ms. Bell?"

"Hey, sorry, I gotta take this."

Teeny called, "Hurry, it's Daisy. She's due back on set in five minutes."

Son of a blue haired donkey! Did I go talk to the devil I knew on the phone, or the one I didn't who was standing in front of me? I chose the lesser of the evils. "Tell her she'll have to call back. I'm busy."

Teeny glared at Palmer and said into the phone, "She's being harassed by the police. Again. Yeah, there was a murder here and..."

I didn't hear the rest because she went into the back room.

"This Daisy must have done something pretty awful to you, if you'd rather talk to me than her." He gave his version of a grin, which was basically just one corner of his mouth turned up. "What'd she do? Run over your cat? Steal your husband?"

"I don't have a cat or a husband," I said, even though that last one was a bit too close to the truth. "She's my youngest sister. What's up?"

"You know anything about the dead body at the gym?"

Here we go. I knew this was coming. "Should I?"

He studied me for a moment. "I'm thinking yes, since you don't seem surprised about a dead body at the gym."

"It's a small town. Word gets around."

"Something tells me the Bell network could rival the CIA. So, I have to ask, do you know anyone who might want Coach Abbott dead?"

"No. I didn't know him well very well, but he always seemed like a good guy. He was my sister's softball coach back when she was in high school, and she came back during summer to help him with softball camp. I need to get back to work now if that is all."

"I'm sorry, it's not all. Have you seen Rowdy recently?" he asked.

"I saw him at Pub Dead a couple of nights ago. But I know that he's missing. My cousin Holly is...uh..." What should I call that relationship? "...friends with him, and she is worried."

He nodded.

"What were you doing up at the school last night?"

"I..."

"And don't lie to me because the security cam caught you going into the gym."

Aunt Tatty and the customer stopped and stared at us.

"Let's go outside." I opened the door, letting the crisp air that had come in with a cold front wash over me. Once we were seated on a bench facing the parked cars in front of the vacant building next to the Merc, I said, "I didn't break in."

"I didn't say you did. The principal let you and your niece in, along with Kira Fry. So yeah, I know you were there when the body was found. What I want to know is *why* you were there."

"I was looking for Nessa."

"Nessa? Coach Anderson." He raised his eyebrows.

"I know you don't believe me, but just because you doubt me doesn't mean it's not true. I wanted to talk to her again."

"So let me get this straight. The ghost of Coach Anderson was just hanging out at the gym?"

"I mean, I don't know that she was just hanging out, but yes, she was there."

"I see. Do you see any spirits here right now?" He crossed his arms over his chest.

"Yeah. There's one leaning against your car." I nodded to the blue Mustang in front of us. The same ghost who showed up with him at my house was back.

"Really." His voice dripped with skepticism. "What does it look like?"

"She is a woman. She's tall, slender, with strawberry blonde hair in two braids, wearing a baseball cap. She has a dimple in her chin. She looks like she could be both the girl next door and a knockout beauty."

He stiffened beside me.

"She has on a pair of white cut-off shorts and a green—"

"Stop."

He stepped off the curb, opened the door of the mustang, and drove off without even so much as a goodbye.

"That was rude," I said aloud.

"It sure was, and I'm here to tell you his Mamma raised him better than that."

I turned to find the Mustang ghost with her hands on her hips, staring in the direction Palmer's car disappeared.

"I'm Lily, by the way," she said.

"Nice to meet you. I'm Star."

"Give him a chance, okay? He's not all that bad."

She disappeared before I could protest or even process what she meant by that.

After work, I dropped Teeny off with Aunt Mer and went and sat with Holly again. Still no news about Rowdy, and it was looking bleak. I ended up sleeping on her couch that night to keep her company and didn't wake until she'd left for work. The whole family would've been there to support her, but she hadn't told anyone else she and Rowdy had been dating.

I was off from all my jobs, so I headed home to get some domestic chores done. I had to haul all the hand-made rag rugs out of the house, upstairs and downstairs. Aunt Maggie had made them on a loom she'd had. I wished I'd gotten to know her before she disappeared. From the stories Granny tells about her, I think she and I would've gotten along well. Hours later, I had all the rugs beaten clean of the accumulated dirt and dust and was tired, hungry, and covered in dust.

I grabbed some cold leftovers and returned to the porch to eat so I wouldn't make too much of a mess. Caroline sat in the porch swing knitting. I wondered if ghosts ever finished their projects and, if so, what they did with them.

I'd just taken a bite of my lunch when the dust at the end of the driveway kicked up. I glanced at my watch. It was too early for Aunt Mer to be home. Soon I recognized Palmer's blue mustang making its way up the long drive-way. What in the world was he doing here?

WITHOUT A WORD about my disheveled state, he said, "You really did see her?"

"Lily? I did." I didn't mention I was looking straight at her right now, too, sitting on the hood of his car.

"What are you?"

I shrugged. "A Bell. We all have gifts. Some are just stranger than others."

"If any of you possess anything stranger than the ability to see dead people, then I'm not sure I want to know about it."

"Nope, I'm the weirdest of the bunch. Now, if you're through insulting me, I'd like to get back to my lunch." I gestured to the plate of lasagna.

"Sorry, I didn't mean to offend you. I've just never met anyone quite like you. But I do have something else to ask of you. I'd like you to come with me and talk to Coach Abbott."

"As I told you at Jessi-Lyn's, it doesn't quite work that way. He won't remember anything about his death."

"He might remember something leading up to it that could help."

"Can it wait? I'm a mess." I indicated my dust covered clothing.

He seemed to notice my appearance for the first time. "Have you been rolling around in the dirt?"

"Something like that."

"So, tell me more about your...what is it you call it? Power?"

"Ability. Some call it a gift, but most of my life I've felt it was a curse."

"Most of your life? How long have you been able to see ghosts?"

"I'd just turned seven and when I first began seeing spirits." Despite the warmth of the sun, I shuddered, remembering my first experience. "My mother was on the stage at the Grand Ole Opry and Astra and I were backstage with her manager, Nevin. A couple of men were standing nearby watching Mamma sing and one said, 'Well, they'll let just about anyone up on stage these days. This is what passes for Country and Western Music now? It's trash is what it is.'

"The other one replied, 'She's trash. You know what I

saw her doing in her dressing room?' I never heard the answer to what Mamma was doing because I stomped over to him and yelled. 'You shut your mouth. My Mamma is not trash!'"

Detective Palmer smiled. "I can see you doing exactly that."

"Yeah, well, it turned out they were both spirits and everyone else only saw me yelling at a curtain. And even worse, Mamma was in between songs and everyone on stage heard me. The two spirits were shocked at my outburst and disappeared, but to me—not being familiar with spirits yet—I thought they'd walked out onto the stage. I ran out there yelling, 'My Mamma is not trash. You take that back! And she sings *weally* good!' Nevin ran out and scooped me up, but I didn't go easily. I was kicking and screaming and trying to escape, but he was a big guy. Astra thought he was hurting me and ran on stage after him, kicking his legs. The audience seemed to think seeing the massive Nevin Arlo being attacked by two tiny girls was hilarious, but Mamma didn't. I didn't learn until much later, it was her very first performance at the Grand Ole Opry and she was never one of those who can laugh at themselves. She took things much too seriously. She was barely able to finish her performance and got bad reviews later because of it. One critic even said the best part of the show was me."

"I bet you were."

I snorted. "A week later we were in the car driving back to Texas. We thought we were just visiting Aunt Mer, but Mamma left us there with her."

"I'm so sorry," Palmer said.

I shoved a bite of lasagna in my mouth. "It is what it is. The worst part was that she punished Astra for my antics. She sent away a three-year-old for doing nothing except trying to protect her big sister."

"And you were only trying to defend your mother," he said. "Did you ever explain to her what you saw and why you ran on stage?"

"Yeah, but Ruby Dee Bell calls reasons excuses. She didn't care why I did it. All she cared about was that I ruined her performance."

"Doesn't seem like you permanently ruined her career. My parents had all your Mamma's albums and used to dance in their living room to *Starlight Above*. I used to complain about how gross they were, two adults dancing. But as I got older, it gave me hope that I'd someday have what they had."

"Did you ever get it? What they had?" I asked.

"For a little while," he said. Then shook his head. "It wasn't meant to be."

Lily. She must have been his girlfriend.

We sat in silence for a few moments, then he said, "You finish your lunch and get that shower you were talking about, then meet me up at the school, okay?"

Lily hopped off the hood of his car. "Dusty James Palmer. Where are your manners?"

She took the words right out of my mouth, but I grinned. "Dusty James, eh?"

"What?"

"Lily called you out for being rude."

He ducked his head. "Sorry about that."

"You apologizing to me or her?"

"Both. I don't know where my manners are." He rubbed the back of his neck. "This case. It's just...it's a lot. I'd appreciate your help if you feel up to it."

I nodded. I wouldn't mind asking Coach Abbott why he was talking about Astra to Nessa.

"Oh, and please and thank you. With sugar on top."

Lily laughed at that. "Tell him not to forget the sprinkles."

I repeated what she said, and his face transformed, making him look like a sad, lost boy. He must have loved her a lot. Or still did, I guess because he said barely above a whisper, "to the moon and back," then got into his car and left without another word.

Freshly showered, but not at all relaxed, I pulled into a visitor parking space at the school. School had already let out for the day, and with the game tonight being an away game—which I only knew because I'd passed the bus loads of loud football fans rolling out of town—the parking lot was empty except for a grey four-door sedan. I sat and waited for Palmer and after a few minutes I got a text from him. "Are you coming?"

I replied, "Yes, I'm already here, in the parking lot. Where are you?"

Palmer texted back, "I'm in the gym. I parked out back."

I stepped down from my Jeep and found Sadie marching across the parking lot toward me with keys in hand and her purse on her shoulder. She looked as stressed as ever, but as she slowed, she smoothed her hair and greeted me with a smile. "What are you doing up here, hon?"

"I'm headed out to the gym," I said.

"It's off limits while the investigation is going on." She opened her car door.

"It's okay. Detective Palmer is meeting me here."

She narrowed her eyes. "For what purpose?"

I wanted to tell her it was none of her business, but I didn't think she'd ever let me out of there if I didn't give her something. "I can talk to the dead. He wants me to see if Coach Abbott can tell me anything about his death."

Sadie paled, and her hand went to her throat. "You can really do that? Talk to Jake? I mean, I knew your family was…"

That unfinished sentence hung in the air for a moment.

"I wish I could talk to Jake just one more time. Our marriage ended badly, and we didn't talk much all these years, even though we worked on the same campus. You always think you have time to make amends and then... you don't."

Her voice broke and she sat down hard on the driver's seat.

Oof! I was so insensitive. This was someone she'd loved at one time. I opened my mouth to apologize but her car door slammed shut.

After Sadie drove away, I made my way out to the gym and found Palmer pacing the floor in front of the bottom row of the bleachers. He stopped when I appeared.

"Sorry, it took me a while. Hope you weren't waiting too long. Sadie stopped me in the parking lot."

"You told Sadie what we were doing?" Palmer scowled.

I nodded. "I didn't know it was a secret."

"It's not. I..." He ran a hand through his hair. "But using a medium isn't exactly sanctioned by the department."

"Well, good thing I'm not a medium then." I grinned.

chapter
twenty-eight

WE SEARCHED THE COACHES' office, the locker rooms, and the baseball diamond with no luck so our next stop was Coach Abbott's mother's house.

"Mrs. Abbott, do you know anyone who would want your son dead?" Palmer sat next to me among at least a dozen crocheted pillows on a sofa covered in floral slipcover with a glass of iced tea in his hand. He'd introduced me as a consultant and after a tour of the house—with no sign of Coach Abbott—we returned to the living room, where Mrs. Abbott had insisted on iced tea and pecan pie. My teeth ached after just one sip of Mrs. Abbott's tea and would probably fall out if I dared taste the pie.

She dabbed her eyes. "I can't think of anyone who'd hurt Jake. I mean, it's just so hard to think anyone I know would even be capable of such a thing. I'm thinking it's gotta be one of those tourists. I remember when Dead

End was just a town, and not a tourist attraction. So, it must be one of those people, because there's good folks in this town. In fact, the only person Jake ever had any real trouble with is his ex-wife. But she's not a murderer. Just a troubled woman."

He flipped through his notes and, apparently coming up empty, said, "Who was he married to?"

"Sadie Kendall. She's the secretary down at the high school," Mrs. Abbott said.

I had to agree with her. Sadie couldn't be capable of murder. Plus, she'd seemed so upset earlier talking about him. But I kept my mouth shut like Palmer had instructed me before we got out of his truck.

"When you say troubled, what do you mean?"

"She believed awful things about my Jake. Things he'd never ever do."

Helen seemed to be avoiding meeting my eyes. I knew her by name and face, but we'd never exchanged more than a few polite words over the years, so this was puzzling.

"What did she believe about him?" Palmer asked.

Her face flushed. "It's too awful to say, really. And it doesn't matter because it certainly isn't true. He would have told me. My son wasn't an angel. Heaven only knows I had a ton of trouble out of him after his father died, but that was small stuff when he was young, and never anything that would hurt anyone."

Palmer put his pen in his notebook and closed it, then leaned forward. "Mrs. Abbott, I'm not here to judge, and neither is my associate. I know this is difficult, but anything you can share with us might lead somewhere. Even if Sadie had nothing at all to do with this, you never know what useful information might be found."

"You have to understand. She was quite...emotional back then. She was on some kind of medicine to help her get pregnant." She took a deep breath and the fluttering of her hands ceased. "She accused him of having an affair."

That didn't sound so bad. I mean, sure, infidelity wasn't something to be praised for, but she'd made it sound like he'd been accused of scalping puppies and wearing them as coats.

"An affair?" Palmer seemed to be as confused as I was.

"Yes. With...with one of his students." She looked straight at me when she said that last word.

To his credit, Palmer's expression didn't change at all.

I shook my head so hard it took me a second to focus. "Not me," I blurted.

"No, not her," Mrs. Abbott whispered. "Her sister Astra."

"That's ridiculous and completely untrue," I insisted.

"I know it is, dear." She leaned over and patted my hand. "I know my son. He would never behave inappropriately with a student. It doesn't matter whether they'd graduated or not. Which is why it crushed him when

Sadie brought it up again recently. He'd thought they'd gotten past all that."

"Recently?" Palmer reopened his notebook and picked up his pen.

"Yes. She was convinced, even back then, that he fathered Astra's daughter."

I laughed then. "That is the most absurd thing I've ever heard. No offense to your son. But why would Sadie think that? Astra was living in Nashville when Teeny was born."

"Jake said it was because he and Astra spent so much time together, and many late nights because of the big tournaments over in Round Rock.

"I remember that. Astra came home from college to help. She didn't get home sometimes until midnight. But that doesn't mean anything," I said.

"He said Sadie was always waiting up for him and demanding to sniff him to see if he smelled like...another woman. Then your sister apparently left town suddenly. She went on the road with your Mamma, right Star?"

I nodded.

"And then after the poor girl—bless her heart—went off the bridge and your mamma brought Astra's baby back to town, Sadie lost it. Those drugs weren't helping her a bit, only making her crazy. She never got pregnant."

She dabbed her eyes again and took a sip of her tea.

"Jake said that was the beginning of the end for them. A few months later, they divorced."

"How tragic." I never knew any of that about Sadie. I'd never seen her anything but calm and helpful.

"Now here I am, a widow with a dead son, and no grandchildren. What am I gonna do with myself?" Her voice broke then.

"I'm so sorry." I squeezed her hand. I hurt for her. And I was angry. Here were people like Mrs. Abbott, who'd give anything to spoil a grandchild. Just one. And then there's my Mamma, who barely acknowledged hers existed and abandoned her own children.

After a few moments, Mrs. Abbott sniffed loudly, dabbed her eyes, and looked directly at me. "That's why I know if any of the rumors were true about him being the father of her baby—your niece—Jake would've told me. He knew how badly I wanted a grandchild, and even if he had hidden it from Sadie, he wouldn't have kept it from me. Besides, that girl is too pretty to have come from Jake. Bless his heart. Any child that came from him would certainly inherit that high forehead of his. He got that from his father. You Bell girls are all so pretty."

"You said Sadie brought up the past again recently?" Palmer asked.

"Yes, last week he said she came into his office and started accusing him all over again and said she had proof he was the father of that baby girl because of his initials and something about a voodoo doll. None of it made sense to me."

Palmer raised his eyebrows and met my glance.

I asked the obvious. "His initials? JA?"

"No. Jake's father wanted to name him after his own father. Nathan. I told Carl—that was my husband—that Jake could be Nathan on all the legal documents, but that name would never pass my lips when I addressed him. We gave him the name Jake for my favorite brother. Nathan Jake Abbott, and we called him Jake, of course. But officially his initials are NA."

NA? It couldn't be. Kira had said they were trying to find Teeny's father. I thought again about the vision I had where Coach Abbott was telling Nessa about his and Astra's shared love of the Atlanta Braves. Had they shared more than that?

"But, Detective, I can't imagine Sadie would kill him over something that happened years ago. Would she? But then again, that family of hers...except Rowdy. He loved that boy like he was his own. Is it true what they're saying? They suspect Rowdy of killing my Jake?"

I didn't hear Palmer's reply because I was plunged into another vision. *I sat beside Rowdy on a bench inside a gym of some kind. His face was stone, but his voice trembled with anger. "...when we got to the cabin, my dad's truck wasn't there. And later when I asked him about it, he told me I was seeing things. I swore to him I didn't. We got into a shouting match, and he hit me. I went down the next day and enlisted and didn't look back."*

Then I was someplace else. Outside. The warm air rolled across my skin as the moon shone on the lake beyond us. I swung my legs on the edge of the dock and looked to my right, where Rowdy sat beside me. He said, "I don't know why Aunt Sadie boarded up the cabin. This place used to be so full of life and the parties Uncle Jake threw here for his players. The last one I was at ended badly, though. Aunt Sadie accused him of sleeping with one of his students. She threw a glass at him, and he ducked, but I was behind him, and it hit me instead."

"Who was the student?" I asked.

"Astra Bell."

A shiver ran down my spine. "What year was this?"

"It was the year before I left for bootcamp, so 2007, I guess? But it wasn't true. First, I know my Uncle Jake. He'd never do that. And also, because..."

The lake disappeared and the brightness of the room blinded me for a moment.

"...but as I said, I just don't see Sadie doing this. You should check out those tourists," Mrs. Abbott said.

Palmer said, "Thank you for your time, Mrs. Abbott. And thank you for letting us look around earlier. Do you know of any other places..."

Color flooded his face, and he rubbed the back of his neck. I could tell he was trying to figure out how to ask where else to look for Jake's spirit without saying that.

"Do you know any place Jake liked to go? Maybe somewhere that was his happy place? Perhaps some place one of those tourists might have followed him to?" I offered.

Palmer shot me a grateful look.

"Well, now, there's only one place that was his happy place, as you call it, and that's the lake."

"Did he have a cabin out there?"

"No, well he did, and they spent a lot of time there when they were married, but she got it in the divorce. He's renting a dock from one of the neighbors so he can keep his boat out there."

Mrs. Abbott walked us to the door, and we said our goodbyes, and climbed into his car but neither of us spoke for a while. I'm not sure what Palmer was thinking about, but I was lost in the vision I'd had. The dock where Rowdy and Nessa had been, that had to be the cabin Mrs. Abbott was talking about. I'd been there myself before.

Palmer pulled off the road into a gas station and turned to me. "Has anything in any of these supernatural encounters you're having pointed to Sadie Kendall?"

I thought about that for a moment. I wasn't sure what to tell him about the latest vision. I still needed to think about it myself. So instead, I said, "I can't imagine Sadie murdering anyone, but can I ask you something?"

"Sure."

"Carly said they found Rowdy's name written in blood next to Coach Abbott's body. Why are you searching for other suspects?" I knew Rowdy wasn't the murderer, but I wanted to know why Palmer wasn't involved in the manhunt with the rest of the department.

He took a deep breath and stared somewhere beyond the hood of his car. He let the breath out slowly, then turned to me with a look on his face that said he'd made up his mind about something. "There was no blood on his hands. Someone else wrote Rowdy's name."

"Who?"

"I don't know yet, but I think someone has gone to a lot of trouble to make it look like Rowdy is the guilty party. And I think whoever was responsible for this murdered Nessa as well."

I remembered what he'd said the day of the parade. *If I didn't believe the truth had been discovered, I wouldn't stop until it was.* You never thought Nessa's death was an accident, did you? You've been secretly investigating this whole time."

He nodded. "You can't share this with anyone. If this goes as far as I think it does, you could put your whole family in danger."

"Why did you ask me about Sadie, earlier? Do you think she is involved in this?"

"I don't know, but I'm going to drop you off and then go have a talk with her."

"Drop me off? Why can't I go?"

"I brought you along with me to Mrs. Abbott's to see if you could see Jake Abbott. I can't take you to question a suspect, Star."

"You just called me Star and not Ms. Bell." I smiled despite the headache that was creeping up the base of my skull.

"Don't get used to it. And don't get used to following me around town."

"I wouldn't dream of it."

twenty-nine

PALMER DROPPED me back at my Jeep and promised to update me when he had any information. But as it was, he didn't call until the next afternoon.

"Sadie has multiple alibis for the night Coach Anderson died. She was at the Junior Varsity football game. And guess who one of her alibis was?" he asked.

"Who?"

"Jessi-Lyn. She was helping chaperone the dance afterward, and she came into the concession stand for change as well during the game."

"What about when Coach Abbott died?" I asked.

"She was at book group with several other witnesses. And your Aunt Merilee was one of those."

I have to say I was relieved, because I didn't like the thought of someone I'd known my whole life and who seemed totally normal turning out to be a killer. But if not her, then who? The visions were making no sense. Even trying to see them from a different perspective, as Granny had suggested. "We need to go out to the lake to see if we can find Coach Abbott out there and talk to him."

"You leave that to me. But do me a favor and just lie low, okay? Quit running around trying to solve this yourself like some real-life Agatha Drew!"

Despite the gravity of the situation, I burst out laughing.

"This is not funny, Star. You have to be careful."

When I finally caught my breath, I said, "You don't read much, do you?"

"Why do you say that?"

"Agatha Christie is an author who wrote mysteries. And Nancy Drew is a character in a mystery series."

"I'm hanging up now. Stay safe."

I'd spent the morning working at the Merc but headed next door to Pub Dead to talk to Zeke about what Mrs. Abbott had said about Astra. He worked with Astra at Jerry's that summer. He might remember if Coach Abbott came to pick her up from work or hung around a lot. I didn't get a chance to even open my mouth before Zeke stalked toward me, pointed to the stairs, and said, "We need to talk. *Now*. About my daughter."

I'd never heard that tone in his voice toward me. Toward anyone. But I got it. Kira had been so distraught the other day about the body in the gym and it was my fault she'd been there. It felt like I'd been stabbed in the chest—not because he was angry with me—but because I wanted someone, just once, to be that angry on my behalf.

"Sure, let's get this over with." I followed him to his apartment.

When we got there, he only paced like a caged animal. He opened his mouth a couple of times but closed it again, as if he were trying so hard to keep control.

"Don't hold back on my account. I deserve every bit of your anger."

He stopped and turned to me, his face morphing into pain instead of anger. "So, you knew?"

"Knew? No, I mean, I should've made the girls stay at home, but I had no idea we'd be finding a body."

Zeke took a breath so deep I could hear it from where I perched on a stool near the door. He let it out before he sank to the bed. "You had no idea. I should have known. You would've never kept her from me on purpose."

"Kept who?"

"My daughter. Teeny."

"Teeny? *Your* daughter?"

"You didn't know." It was a statement, not a question, and more like a life preserver he was clinging to. "I'm sorry. I didn't..." He buried his face in his hands.

I shot off the stool and went to the bed and sat beside him. "Why do you think Teeny is yours?"

"I wondered. But it was just the once."

"No." I stood up. "You and Astra? Y'all were never. She wouldn't...not with you, especially."

"Thanks a lot." He let out a bitter laugh.

"No, I mean. You...back then...you went from one girl to another. Astra would've never been just a one-night stand. I know my sister."

"It wasn't a one-night stand." He said between clenched teeth.

"You just said it was just the once."

"We'd been together that whole summer. We didn't...I never touched her until...and then she left town a few days later. Without a word. And then Jessi-Lyn came to me and told me she was pregnant. And I did the right thing and married her."

"The right thing? You were sleeping with Jessi-Lyn at the same time you were seeing my sister?"

"It wasn't like that." He whispered. "I'd ended things with Jessi-Lyn after the first time Astra and I hung out. I found her on the side of the road out of gas. I offered her a ride into town to the nearest gas station. She was hot and mad and yelling at herself for not remembering to fill the tank, so I took a detour on the way back into town to my favorite swimming hole in the woods on the back of the Morton place. Nothing happened. We just swam, but something changed in me that day. Your sister...I tease you about being a witch, but your sister was pure magic. You know how I was back then, you already said it. I...got around. But I didn't want it to be that way with Astra. It was like going from being a deer hunter to sighting a deer in the woods and wanting to melt into the tree, so you didn't scare it away."

I didn't want to hear this. But I had a feeling he was no longer talking to me directly.

"We hung out nearly every day. Late at night, mostly after we both got off work. We'd lay in the bed of my truck and stare up at the stars and talk about what we both wanted from life. And what kept us going in the present. We held hands, and that was it. Then one day we went back to that swimming hole. We ended up skinny dipping. And then...it happened. And it was beautiful and nothing like I'd ever experienced. Then she left. Without a word. It hurt like hell."

I squeezed his hand. "I'm sorry. I know the pain of being left behind."

He looked up at me then, as if realizing I was still there. "Yeah, I could see on your face what I felt right after she left. Just as I could see the joy when she returned."

Tears filled my eyes. Our joy had been short-lived.

"I blamed myself for her leaving," he said. "I replayed every moment in the lake. Had I taken things too fast? Had I done something wrong?"

I thought about that for a moment. "I don't think you did. You said that right after Astra left, Jessi-Lyn told you she was pregnant. Maybe she'd already told Astra, and that's why Astra left? She didn't want to hurt Jessi-Lyn."

"I don't know. Maybe."

"But then, when she found out she was pregnant, why didn't she tell me? Was I that horrible of a person she didn't want our daughter to know me?"

"I don't know. I mean, no, you are definitely not a horrible person. I don't know what went through her mind back then, but Zeke…" I paused, trying to figure out exactly how to say this. "Please don't take this the wrong way, but are you sure there was no one else Astra was with?"

He opened his mouth to speak and shut it again, opened it once more, then shook his head. "I knew her, Star. You knew her."

"I thought I knew her."

"If she was with anyone else during that time, I would've known."

"But the voodoo doll. The initials NA," I insisted.

Zeke opened his mouth again to speak, but I held up a hand. "And there's something else. She spent a lot of time with Coach Abbott that summer and—"

"Coach Abbott? You think your sister would date a married man? And one twenty years older than her? Star, come on."

I told him what Mrs. Abbott said about Sadie and ended with. "And your initials are ZF, not NA."

He laughed then. That hearty golden laugh that had made me first fall in love with him in the ninth grade. I didn't see what was funny. Maybe this was all too much for him and he was losing his mind. He'd carried a torch for Astra for years and to find out now she'd gotten pregnant by her softball coach. It was too much. He continued to cackle and was bent over double. So, I continued, "And Mrs. Abbott said Coach Abbott didn't get home until way past practice every night and I remember how Astra would come home past midnight herself and—"

"She was with me, Star." His laughter finally stopped. "And I'm NA. Those aren't initials for someone's name. It stood for Nice Ass."

My eyes went straight to his butt. I mean, he did have a rather fabulous ass.

"That's what clued me in. When the girls were here after you brought them over after the gym, and they talked about the initials. Plus, what Astra said to Jessi-Lyn, 'some mistake I made on the road' We joked a lot that if she hadn't run out of gas, we might not have ended up together. And she called me the best mistake on the road she'd ever made."

"You're really Teeny's dad?" Tears filled my eyes. Teeny had a father. I'd never wanted to share her with anyone else, and I dreaded the day when some dead-beat musician showed up and tried to take her from me, but Zeke would never do that. Zeke was family.

"And Teeny's nose. I don't know how I didn't see it before. I mean, I did. I always thought there was something so familiar about her, but I just figured it was because she looked like Astra. But it wasn't. Not entirely." He walked over to his dresser and picked up a frame holding a faded photo of a young woman. "This was my mother when she was young. Check out her nose."

It was a freckled, upturned nose, the spitting image of Teeny's. Nothing else looked like her, but that nose I saw every day of my life for the past fourteen years. I smiled. Then a sudden thought occurred to me. "That's why Astra went straight to Jessi-Lyn when she came back. She wanted to tell her about Teeny before she told anyone else."

"Even me?" The hurt in his eyes was almost unbearable. I reached out and touched his arm.

"You know Astra and what she valued. You two did nothing wrong before she left; you and Jessi-Lyn weren't together. But when she came back and you and Jessi-Lyn were married—with a kid, for Pete's sake—she needed to break the news to Jessi-Lyn herself. They were best friends long before you were anything with either of them. She owed that to Jessi-Lyn."

"That sounds just like her. She was always putting the needs of others before her own."

"And I bet you anything, her next stop was you."

"But she died before..." Zeke's phone vibrated in his

pocket. He pulled it out and glanced at the screen, and his smile brightened even more. "Hey baby girl! What's up?"

The sound on the other end was so loud I heard it from where I was standing. Before I could register that it was hysterical crying, Zeke had grabbed his wallet and keys and had flown down the stairs. He was in his truck and gone before I even got to the sidewalk. Just then, my own phone rang. Aunt Mer's face lit up the display. My heart sped up.

"Is Teeny hurt?" I asked as soon as I pushed the answer call button. "No, honey, she's here with me. She wasn't with Kira. But we're on our way to the hospital and I just wanted to let you know where we were."

"Hospital? You said she wasn't hurt."

"She's not. Jessi-Lyn and Kira were in an accident, and Kira called Teeny, begging her to come up to the hospital and, of course, Teeny wanted to be by her side. There was no reasoning with the girl, so that is where we are headed. Just wanted you to know. I need to hang up and drive now so we don't get in an accident ourselves."

The phone went silent, and I jumped into my Jeep and headed over to the hospital.

When I arrived, the ER waiting room was full of people I knew. Zeke was talking to Carly quietly in the corner. Aunt Mer and Teeny were seated against the windows.

Aunt Mer rose when she saw me. She gave me a quick hug and excused herself to go to the restroom. I took her chair and then Teeny looked up and relief filled her face.

"She refused to leave me alone in the waiting room. She probably would've peed on herself here in this chair if you hadn't come."

"Have you heard anything about Jessi-Lyn and Kira?" I asked. "How are they?"

"They're mostly okay. Kira has some cuts and bruises, but Jessi-Lyn's arm is broken." Teeny talked while texting on her phone. "Kira says they are wheeling her to x-ray now."

Relief flooded me. If Kira was well enough to text, she was going to be okay. I glanced toward where Carly and Zeke had been talking, but they'd both disappeared. "Did Kira say what happened?"

"She said it was someone in a big truck who ran them off the road. She said it had those big spotlights on the top."

Rowdy's truck? Not possible.

"Probably some jerk from THS who saw the DEHS bumper stickers all over Jessi-Lyn's car. It's the big rivalry next week," Teeny said.

Aunt Mer came back then with an armful of snacks from the vending machine. She doled out a couple of packages to Teeny and offered me some, but I shook my head. "I'm gonna go see if I can find Carly."

Something wasn't sitting right with me, and I had to talk to her. I walked all up and down the hall and even peeked into the chapel, but there was no sign of either her or Zeke. Just as I was about to give up, my phone buzzed in my pocket. It was Zeke.

"Hey, Jessi-Lyn wants to talk to you," he said.

"To me? Why?"

"She's kind of loopy—they've given her morphine for the pain—and she said that you were the only one she could trust with her big secret."

"Okay, I'll come on back. Will they let me through into the patient area?"

"Hold on, I'm coming out."

He led me through the flurry of uniformed medical personnel flitting back and forth between the curtained areas to the back where Jessi-Lyn lay with her arm in a sling. From the doorway, she looked so small and frail. Not at all like the fiery woman I'd come to know and sometimes hate. Most of my anger toward her had fizzled out over the past few days while helping her with Nessa. And the rest was extinguished when she opened her eyes and her face crumpled. She reached her good arm out to me. "Star. You came!"

But she wasn't alone. Nessa stood at the head of her hospital bed.

chapter
thirty

ZEKE LEANED IN AND WHISPERED, "I'll leave you to it. I'm gonna go see if there's any update on Kira's x-rays."

Tears rolled down Jessi-Lyn's cheeks. Once Zeke closed the door behind him, she started in with, "I was so scared I was going to lose my baby. And I know you said you didn't put a curse on me, but I *feel* cursed, Star. And I think the only way to break it is to tell you everything."

"Oh darling," Nessa crooned. "You need to rest."

"I agree," I said to Nessa.

Jessi-Lyn said, "So, there is a curse?"

"No, sorry, I was talking to Nessa. She said you need to rest."

"Nessa is here?" Jessi-Lyn asked. "In my room? Where?"

I nodded to the spot at the head of the bed. "There."

Jessi-Lyn sobbed in her hands. "I wish she could hold me and tell me it's going to be okay. I miss her so much."

"She misses you too," I said. "I didn't have to hear the words from Nessa. They were written all over her face.

Jessi-Lyn gripped my hand. "It's all my fault. Every bit."

"What's your fault?"

"Ev-er-y-thing!" She emphasized each syllable. "All the way back to Astra's death."

Yeah, it was, I thought reflexively. But I wasn't so sure I still meant it. "You loved Astra. I know you would never hurt her on purpose. Accidents happen. Y'all were young and stupid and driving too fast."

"I left her there," Jessi-Lyn whispered. "At the lake."

I patted her hand. "You were unconscious. You couldn't have saved her."

"No, you don't understand! She wasn't in the car with me. She never was. Not when I went off the bridge," Jessi-Lyn insisted.

This wasn't the morphine talking.

Her next words came out in a rush. "We got into a fight there at the lake. I drove off and left her there. But Star, I swear I didn't remember it after the accident. The one back then. I promise. I didn't! Not until Nessa and I were out at the lake for Labor Day last month. And it's the reason I broke up with Nessa because she was poking into things and—"

I held up a hand to Jessi-Lyn and turned to Nessa. "Nessa, tell me the very last thing you remember before you died."

"I told you, Labor Day weekend."

"No, I mean specifically from that weekend."

She left Jessi-Lyn's bedside and paced. "I remember packing the car, driving to Jess' house. We dropped Kira off with her dad. Maybe that was the last thing? Wait, no, I remember gassing up, and then we went over the lake on the bridge, and that's when Jess started hyperventilating. I should've pulled over then, but I didn't. Not until we got to Samson Farm Road. She was sobbing by that time, so I pulled over. She jumped out and threw up in a ditch. I held her hair back and in between dry heaves, she just kept crying and saying, "I remember. I remember. Oh my God, what did I do? I kept asking her what she remembered. And finally, she told me what she just told you, about fighting with Astra and leaving her there at the lake."

I turned back to Jessi-Lyn. "Where did you leave her? What part of the lake?"

"Over there off Samson Farm Road," Jessi-Lyn said dreamily. The drugs were kicking in.

The police had searched the lake, and even along the banks near the bridge in case Astra had washed ashore, but her body was never found. Because they searched the wrong place the whole time.

"And the very last thing you remember is her confession?" I asked Nessa.

"No, I uh..." she ran a hand through her hair. "I told her she had to go to the police because they'd been looking in the wrong place. She freaked out then and said she couldn't go to the police because they'd ask her what the fight was about. She asked me to stop talking about it and to take her home."

I felt a whole new surge of anger rise in me. An accident was one thing, but abandoning my sister there at the lake? And then to keep it from us once she remembered. I wanted to storm out of there and leave Jessi-Lyn believing she was cursed. But that would make me no different from Jessi-Lyn. Maybe that's why we never got along. We were too much alike—hot tempered and stubborn. While Astra was the cool balm that soothed us both.

"Did you take her home?" I asked Nessa.

"I did. I think. I don't remember reaching the house. I...the last thought I remember having was that I could fix this. I would search for Astra myself. That way, I could give your family closure and keep Jessi-Lyn out of it."

"That is the very last thing you remember? Nothing else."

She shook her head. "Nothing more. I'm sorry. I don't know what happened after that. Only what Jess just told you. She broke up with me because I was looking into things. So, I guess I decided to tell her instead of keeping it a secret?"

"I am not so sure you did tell her. She thought you were cheating on her with Rowdy Kendall, but I think he was helping you look into things."

I told her about the visions.

"Rowdy Kendall? From Krav Maga? I barely know him."

"Apparently you got closer. And I'm thinking maybe that's what got you killed." And why he's missing. "You got too close to the truth."

"What truth?"

"That's what I need to figure out. I gotta go."

Instead of going to the waiting room, I turned at the last minute and headed out through the side door. I needed time to think without all the people around. I needed to figure this out. I made my way to the fountain and benches that were set among a copse of trees on the south side of the hospital. I'd first found it when Aunt Willa Jo had been in labor with the twins. I sat and stared at the gurgling water, letting the calming sound remove everything else from my mind. Astra hadn't died in the accident on the bridge. Her body hadn't floated away on the waters of the lake. She'd gone missing somewhere else. Off Samson Farm Road.

I sat and watched the water and thought about all the visions I'd had. Nessa and Rowdy weren't having an affair.

They were looking into Astra's death. And they were murdered by whoever killed my sister. Coach Abbott was also dead.

I wasn't stupid. I knew who all these people had in common. But Sadie had alibis the nights both Nessa and Coach Abbott were killed. Then I heard the voice again I'd heard in the gym. *"You should've kept your nose out of it. She's dead and no one will ever find her."*

I texted Palmer, "Headed out to the lake cabin to look around. Meet me out there if you can. No time to explain."

I turned onto Samson Farm Road, going over everything in my head. How did I not see it before? Sadie boarded up the cabin. I knew that from the vision. Coach Abbott warned Nessa to stay away from the Kendalls. Rowdy's father denied being at the lake. Sadie did this, but she didn't do it alone.

I hadn't been out this way in years. The last time had been senior year at Coach Abbott's annual end-of-year barbecue for the athletes. Astra dragged me along with her because Jessi-Lyn had mono. I remembered the road leading to his cabin had a weird name. It wasn't an official road, so it wasn't anything I could Google. It had a hand-made sign. Something to do with sports or fishing? Maybe both? I passed it and slammed on my brakes. I put my Jeep in reverse and the sign came into view. It was faded, but I could still read the words.

Third Bass. Painted next to the words was a fish wearing a baseball cap and holding a bat. I would've rolled my eyes at the horrible pun, but I had more urgent matters on my mind.

I traveled down the dirt road as far as I could go until a locked gate appeared in front of me. I could climb it, but I didn't want to leave my car there in case anyone came up. I remembered seeing a small dirt road off to the right, so I turned around and went back the way I came with a sign that said public boat ramp. I could leave my car down there and make my way through the woods to the house. The road was more like a path filled with huge ruts. I bounced around in my seat until I came to a small incline. When I got to the top, the lake appeared over the horizon. It was a beautiful sight, with the sun glistening across the water as it set.

It also blinded me briefly, so I waited until my eyes adjusted and then continued toward the ramp. In the distance, Palmer's blue mustang stood out. He was already here. Relief filled me. I wouldn't have to do this alone.

As soon as I got close enough, I spotted another vehicle. Rowdy's truck. And Rowdy himself stood beside it, looking like he was ready for a fight. Yes! With him and Palmer on my side, I didn't have to do this by myself. Holly would be so relieved he was alive.

"Stop right there," Rowdy said and hovered his hand near his service weapon.

I stopped. And not because Rowdy told me to. It was because a realization had dawned on me. When his hand moved, it shimmered.

thirty-one

JUST AS I knew I could never snuggle up with the blankets Caroline knitted, I knew Rowdy's gun couldn't hurt me. It was on another plane along with him. But I held my hands up anyway. "Rowdy, it's me. Star Bell."

He didn't lower his gun. "What are you doing here?"

I didn't have time for an explanation. I had to get to the point. "You're dead, Rowdy."

"No."

"Yes, you are, and I don't have time to explain. I need your help. Have you seen Palmer?"

"Who?"

"Detective Dusty Palmer with the Ingersoll County Criminal Investigations Division. That's his car." I nodded to the mustang.

"Oh, the new guy over at county? We don't deal with them much unless there is a...homicide."

This was so frustrating. It was like losing power while playing a video game and having to start the level all over.

He lowered his gun but kept his eye on me. "Why are you looking for him?"

"The last thing you remember is agreeing to take Nessa Anderson from your Krav Maga class out to the cabin where your Uncle Jake took you fishing when you were a kid. Am I right?"

He took a step back. I took one forward.

"You saw your dad at the cabin the day my sister and Jessi-Lyn Gibson went off the bridge, but he denied it and y'all got into a huge fight, and you went down and enlisted the next day."

"What...how...I don't..." He clutched his skull with both hands and sank to a squatting position, rocking on his heels. "I haven't seen anyone else. I don't even know how I got here."

"I think your guy is down at the cabin," a voice said behind me.

I whipped around and found Coach Abbott.

"He's in pretty awful shape, though. I think they shot him in the chest."

"Uncle Jake?" Rowdy stood.

Coach Abbott held out his arms and Jake crossed the distance in two steps. "It's gonna be okay, son, I've got ya."

"Who shot him?" I asked. "Sadie?"

"You figured her out, did you? I wondered when someone would. She's made me out to be the bad guy all these years, but she's psychotic. I reckon she's the one who offed me."

At least I didn't have to explain to him he was dead. But I was curious. "What's the last thing you remember?"

"Sitting in my office and hearing a gun cock behind me."

"I need to call the police." I pulled my phone out of my pocket to call Carly.

"There's no cell phone reception out here," Coach Abbott said. "There's a dead zone that reaches all the way out to the road."

"Then I'll have to drive out to the road where I—"

"There's no time for that. He's losing a lot of blood. Sadie is alone for now; you can get up there and overpower her and get the detective out of there before the others arrive."

"With what? The only weapon I have in my car is a pair of nail scissors in the shape of a unicorn," I squeaked.

"You are standing beside two vehicles belonging to cops, Star." Rowdy spread his hands wide. "Between the two of us, I'm sure we have an arsenal."

"Rowdy, you help her out, and I'll go to the cabin and keep an eye on things there," Coach Abbott said. He disappeared. He seemed to get the hang of the ghost thing quicker than the others.

I tried the Mustang, which was locked, and it horrified me thinking of even touching a window in that beautiful car. Much less breaking one. I moved to Rowdy's truck where I had better luck.

"I keep a Glock in there." Rowdy nodded to the glove box. "There's another one under the seat, and I have a shotgun behind the seat."

I unlatched the glove box and pulled out the gun there with shaking hands.

"You've never held a gun before, have you?" Rowdy asked.

It was true. I mean, most of the world probably thinks Texans run around with a gun strapped to the side of their leg, riding their horses around in their ten-gallon hats, but they'd be wrong. Uncle Gavin preferred fishing to hunting, and we never felt the need to protect ourselves in Dead End. Even Boone only kept a baseball bat behind the bar. Uncle Buddy was the only hunter, but I'd never had a reason to get him to teach me to shoot.

I shook my head.

"You're going to get a quick verbal lesson. It would go better if I could show you, but this will have to work."

He rattled off a bunch of stuff, and I tried to pay attention, but it was a lot.

.   .   .

I made my way through the woods, the back way to the cabin, with Rowdy leading the way. The sun had set by then, but the full moon shone in the sky lighting my path.

The lights illuminated the house. And there was a white truck sitting beside Sadie's sedan. She had help.

"That's my dad's truck. Sonofabitch."

We made a wide circle around the house, ending up on the northwest corner. Now that I was here, I wasn't at all sure what I was supposed to do.

"Wait here and let me check things out." He disappeared before I could acknowledge her command.

He and Coach Abbott reappeared as I crouched behind a tree. "They've got him upstairs. They're in the kitchen arguing, but I think you can sneak past them if you go in through the side door."

I opened the door as quietly as I could and took the stairs immediately to the right. The stairs creaked under my weight, but they never heard me over their arguing. I recognized both voices. Sadie and her brother, Mayor Kendall. I was too rushed to hear much of what they said, but I caught Sadie's, "You told me to handle it and I did!"

I located Palmer immediately and not finding a lock on the door; I wedged a chair under the doorknob. They could break it down with any amount of force, but it would slow them down a bit.

Once my eyes adjusted to the dark, I saw Palmer

huddled in the corner. Lily was by his side. If the look on her face was any indication, he was in terrible shape.

"Hey, Dusty. How are you doing, buddy?" I whispered.

He was shivering and sweat beaded on his upper lip.

"Having visions now. That's how I'm doing."

"Visions? Ghosts? You can see Lily?"

"No, you. I know you're not really here. But it's nice to see you, even in my imagination." He closed his eyes again.

"Please help him," Lily said.

I nodded and shrugged out of my jacket and put it over Palmer. I sat back against the wall beside him with the gun pointed at the door. "If this is your imagination, it's pretty lame, man. If you're gonna imagine being rescued, you should've imagined a whole posse. But a scared-shit-less witch with a gun she doesn't know how to operate, and three ghosts is all you've got, my dude."

He managed a small laugh that turned into a terrible coughing fit. He held his ribs and once he caught his breath, he said, "You have to take the safety off."

"Yeah, I was, uh, about to do that," I lied. Rowdy had said something about a safety.

"You've never used a gun, have you?"

"Do video games count?" I thought of the many nights Grey, Carly, and I sat up playing Grey's PS3.

"Not unless you're planning to shoot your tv. Let me see it." He sounded a bit more alert.

I handed it to him, knowing enough to hand it to him handle first. Although I didn't think handle was the right term for the end of the gun. He took it from me, examined it, did a little clicky thing that slid out a cartridge, popped it back in, and pointed it at the door. "Where did you get these?"

I told him about Rowdy and Abbott. "That's how I knew where you were."

He nodded. "Are they here now?"

"No, but Lily is." I nodded in her direction.

He smiled. "Of course she is. She never leaves my side, does she?"

I felt a pang in my chest I couldn't quite explain. I couldn't imagine having someone who loved you so much they stayed by your side even in death.

"Not when he is doing bathroom stuff. Make sure he knows that. I give him his privacy. I always have," Lily said.

I told him what she said, and he laughed, which triggered another coughing fit. He held his side. "Tell her I appreciate that."

I glanced at the blood on his arm where he'd coughed into it. "We need to get you out of here and get you some help!"

"Too late for that now." Rowdy appeared in front of

me. "They've brought back up and the back stairs are blocked. I'm sorry, but you're both trapped. Star, you're gonna have to use my gun."

Palmer looked at me. "Take the gun. Show me you know how to hold it. Make sure your thumb isn't in the way or it's gonna get knocked off when you discharge it."

He had me practice a few times aiming, but with my hand off the trigger.

"You don't put your finger on the trigger unless you plan to shoot, you got it?"

I nodded.

"And don't worry about aiming for their heads. The chest is a bigger target. This caliber will take them down if you hit them anywhere in the torso. Now hand me the other gun."

I did as he said, and he went through the motions with that one the same as he did the first. Then let it rest in his hand and closed his eyes again. After a moment he said, "How did you know to come look for me here?" he asked.

"I didn't. I had no idea you were here. But after talking to Jessi-Lyn in the hospital, I—"

"What happened to Jessi-Lyn?"

"Someone ran her off the road. And she told me that Astra was never in the car with her when it went off the bridge. Apparently, they'd had a fight, and she left Astra at the lake. Then I realized what part of the lake, and where Astra would've gone to."

"Here? Why?"

"She knew the area. Coach Abbott always had end of the year parties here for his athletes. She was here every year. So, when Jessi-Lyn described the area they had the argument, I knew she would go to Coach Abbott's cabin."

"And you connected Sadie because of what Mrs. Abbott said about their fights back then."

"Well, I kind of got to that. But I also had another vision when we were there. I didn't know what to make of it, so I didn't mention it then. But what sealed it is when Jessi-Lyn said she and Nessa broke up because Nessa wouldn't stop looking into things. That's why Sadie killed Nessa. She got close. And Rowdy, he was helping her. Then I started thinking about all the visions. How Coach Abbott warned Nessa to stay away from the Kendalls."

Heavy footfalls sounded on the stairs outside and raised voices indicated more than one person was coming. I lifted the gun with shaky hands.

Palmer said, "Change of plans. Hide in that closet. If they shoot me, you hide here until they're gone. Quick."

I didn't question him. I just scrambled across the floor and shut the door just as the bedroom door opened. I was shaking so badly and my heart was pounding so fast I just knew they could hear it.

"What the hell is this?" A man shouted and something

clattered on the floor. The chair that had been up against the doorknob. "You think that's gonna keep us out?"

It was the mayor. Except now he didn't have his smarmy public voice. He was pissed. "My guy found a Jeep parked down the road where your truck is. My sister says it belongs to one of the Bell witches—the one who sees ghosts. Where is she?"

Palmer said, "Beats me. I've been a bit busy here trying not to die."

Mayor Kendall said, "Something tells me purple isn't your color."

My jacket. I'd left it out there. I didn't think, I just pointed the gun at the door. I wasn't going to die today, or if I did, I was taking this son of a bitch down with me.

Kendall jerked open the door and the light flooded the closet, blinding me temporarily. I pulled the trigger, hoping I was hitting him, but nothing happened. I'd forgotten the safety. Once Kendall realized what I'd done, he jerked the gun out of my hand, grabbed me by the hair, drug me out of the closet, and tossed me on the floor beside Palmer. I looked up and found Briggs standing next to him.

Kendall handed him the gun I'd tried to use on him and said, "Take care of both of them."

He left and I heard him yelling down the stairs at Sadie to make him a drink.

"You can't do this, Paul." I used his first name instead

of his title on purpose. "How are you ever going to face Carly? You know she will never stop looking for me."

"I'm doing this *for* her."

"Killing her best friend? How is that for her?"

"You're not gonna change his mind, Star," Palmer grabbed my hand.

Briggs lifted the gun and aimed it at my head. His hand shook slightly. "I never wanted any of this. But it's gone too far. I was only ever trying to protect Carly and Rock."

None of that made sense, but he lowered the gun, so I kept talking. "They adore you. Don't turn their hero into a murderer."

"Too late," he said. He pulled the trigger and shot me.

I'D NEVER FELT SO much pain in my life. My leg was on fire, but the rest of me felt cold.

"Star? Stay with me," Palmer pled.

I moaned. The pain was too much.

"Sorry, I've got to stop the blood flow." I heard fabric rip and then something tight on my leg.

I was shivering, and he put my jacket around me and held me against his chest.

"Talk to me," he said.

"About what?"

"Anything," he said. "Tell me about the most embarrassing thing you ever did."

"This one time...I tried to shoot someone...and left the safety on." I managed to get out between clenched teeth.

His chest vibrated beneath me with a small laugh that

once again turned into a cough. I lifted my head and saw blood seeping from the bullet wound in his shoulder. "What a pair we are."

"Between us, we still have three good arms and three good legs," he smiled weakly.

"That would help us in a potato sack race."

"Yeah, I think the stakes are a bit more serious than that."

I had to agree.

I'm not sure how long we sat like that because I floated in and out of consciousness.

My eyes fluttered open, hearing a soft voice. It was Lily. She sat at Dusty's feet, tears on her face. "I wanna hold you again, baby, but not like this. You have so much more life to live. Please wake up."

I sat up and Dusty toppled over.

"He's stopped breathing," she cried.

The pain in my leg forgotten, I scrambled to him and felt for a pulse. It was slow and faint, but he was still alive. His chest wasn't rising and falling, so I started performing CPR. After what felt like an eternity, he coughed and began breathing. I let out a sob. The pain came flooding back into my leg again and blood seeped through my jeans.

"What happened?" Palmer asked.

"You tried to freaking die on me. Don't you ever do that again. You scared both me and your girl."

"My girl?"

"Lily. She woke me up just in time."

He smiled then. "Lily is my mother."

"Your mother? She's younger than I am."

"She died when I was a kid."

Of course, how had I missed that? The first words she said to me came back. *His Mamma raised him better than that.*

I tried to ignore the spark I felt at knowing he wasn't pining after a dead girlfriend. There was no time for any of that. At all.

Once again, heavy footsteps sounded on the stairs and the door flew open. Kendall pushed Sadie through the doorway, and she stumbled and fell. "You can't do this. I'm your sister, Hank. What would Daddy say?"

"Daddy? He'd have already taken the belt to you, girl. And worse. You know that. I protected you from him. And I got you out of every mess you ever got your fool self in, but that's done. There's only one more mess I'm cleaning up."

He turned his gaze over to us. Palmer put a protective arm around me.

Kendall bellowed, "Paul, I thought I told you to shoot the witch?"

Briggs stood in the doorway. "I did. She should have bled out by now."

"Well, she'll be gone soon enough. You got your cuffs

on you?"

"Yeah, but you're not using them."

"And just why the hell not?" The mayor demanded.

"Hank, don't be an idiot. What do you think is going to happen if anything of mine is found at the scene?"

"Not a damn thing, since you'll be the one investigating it."

"No, I won't. I don't know how you got elected, since you have no idea how things work around here. I am the Sheriff. I don't investigate. We have a department for that. The CID at county will send over their next best detective since you're getting rid of their best one. And if they find someone cuffed here, they're not gonna believe this one is an accident."

"Then it's up to you to figure out how to make it look like one, but for now, cuff Sadie to the bed over there so she won't cause us any trouble while we think."

Briggs uttered a string of expletives but did as Kendall told him.

My heart thumped so loudly in my chest I could barely hear the rest. We were going to die here.

As soon as the door closed behind them, Sadie started trying to pull herself free from the bed. They hadn't tied me or Dusty up. But Dusty wasn't going anywhere, and he was getting pale again. My leg was still on fire, and even the tiniest movement caused pain to shoot from my hip to my toes, so I laid my head back on Dusty.

"Get over here and help me!" Sadie demanded.

"If I could stand up and make it over to you, all I'd do is strangle you with my bare hands, so be glad I can't move."

"If you get me out of here, I can run for help." She bargained.

"And just who is going to help us? You heard your brother. The entire police department is under his control." I thought once again of Carly. What would Briggs tell her when my body was found, or never found? She'd never stop hunting for me.

"This is all your fault, you know. If you hadn't started poking into Nessa's death, then none of this would've happened."

That got my adrenaline pumping. I sat up and glared at her. "Are you fucking delusional Sadie, or just stupid? You started all of this when you murdered my sister."

"It was an accident! I didn't mean to!" she hollered at me. "But if we want to talk about starting stuff. If she hadn't slept with my husband and gotten pregnant, then flaunted their affair by showing up at my cabin in a bikini then—"

"She wasn't sleeping with your husband."

"You know she did. The voodoo doll with the initial N.A. That was for Jake. His full name is—"

"I know his full name, and I know what happened. Zeke is Teeny's father. N.A. stood for Nice Ass. And she showed up at the cabin in a bikini that day because she got into a fight with Jessi-Lyn and Jessi-Lyn left her on the side of the road. She came here for help."

"No. She...no." Sadie slumped to the floor. "She was telling the truth about that? I found her here, and I thought she was lying. She'd been gone a year and then she shows up all over again and I'd found the mojo bag in Jake's truck. I thought...and I pushed her, and she fell, and I didn't mean for it to happen. I panicked."

"What mojo bag?" I went cold all over. "And where is my sister's body?"

Sadie clammed up then. "I'm not telling you anything more. Not until you help me get loose."

"I told you; I can't move. And even if I could get over there, how am I going to get you out of the handcuffs?"

"I have a key," Dusty whispered. "They took my cuffs and gun, but I always keep an extra key in my pocket. Don't ask. There was this situation once...anyway, it's in a hidden pocket, just inside my waistband. If you want to know where your sister is, dig it out."

"She's just going to use it and run. She's not going to help us. We're going to die here."

"But you'll die with closure." Something on his face told me there was something he'd never gotten closure on.

"What are you two whispered about over there?"

"Dusty has a cuff key. I'll give it to you, but I want to know everything about Astra."

"How do I know you're telling the truth?"

I dug out the key and held it up.

"She's in the well," Sadie whispered. "When I realized I'd killed her, I panicked and called Hank. He was a deputy back then. He came right over. He always came running when I needed him. But he couldn't see Astra's body. I thought I was losing my mind, but then I realized the mojo bag really worked. It was for hiding things."

"Back up. What mojo bag? Where did you get it?" I knew the answer. There was only one place in Dead End she could've gotten it.

"As I told you, I found it in Jake's truck when we were cleaning it out to sell it. He denied ever seeing it, so I took it to your Aunt Tatty to ask her what it was for. She wouldn't tell me at first." Sadie laughed bitterly. "But with a little green encouragement, she told me she didn't make it for Jake. She made it for Astra. And with a bit more money, she told me it was for hiding things."

I didn't have time to let that sink in because Sadie continued, "I reached down and plucked the bag off the ground and when I did, Jake could see her. Briggs came up then. Apparently, he'd gotten the call that a car had gone off the bridge. They had to go, but Hank grabbed the mojo bag from me, tossed it on Astra and she disappeared again. He said he'd be back later to take care of it."

"And that's when Uncle Jake and I came back?" Rowdy said.

I turned to him. "The vision I had. You were telling Nessa about it. That's the last fight you had with your dad. The one that made you run off and join the Marines?"

He nodded.

"Who are you talking to?" Sadie demanded.

"Rowdy." That reminded me of something else I needed to get off my chest. "My sister's death might have been an accident, but you murdered three other people."

"That's not how it happened. Nessa was digging into things and asking questions. And I heard her that day at the school, when Teeny and Kira were caught fighting. She and Jessi-Lyn were arguing in the teacher's lounge. I was in the bathroom, and they didn't hear me. Jessi-Lyn accused her of having an affair with Rowdy, but Nessa told her she was looking into Astra's death, and she thought she'd found something. She wanted to meet with her later that night."

"You snuck out of the game and killed her, then went back. That's how you had an alibi. You made sure enough people saw you before and after."

"Yes. Now give me the key."

"And Rowdy got close, and you killed him?"

"No, I didn't. I would never." Tears filled her eyes. "His father did."

Rowdy disappeared then. I didn't blame him. My mother had done awful things, but to think that your own parents could take your life. My heart broke for him.

"Now, will you give me the key? I swear I will run for help," Sadie begged.

I glanced at Palmer. He was paler now, and his breathing was uneven, but at least he *was* breathing. Sadie was a liar and a murderer, but maybe she was telling the truth. If there was any way we could be rescued, I had to change it.

Once again, the door to the room flew open. It startled me and I dropped the cuff key.

Sadie cowered, and Kendall narrowed his eyes. "What's going on in here? You can't really be thinking about escaping, can you? You'd have to dislocate your wrist to get out of those cuffs and then where would you even go? You know your own cabin better than anyone. You'd never survive the fall from that window."

Sadie curled up further into a ball.

"Here, sir." A younger red-headed guy came up behind him. He looked familiar, but I couldn't place him with the pain clouding my head.

"Don't stand there son, you know the plan. Uncuff her." He dug into his pocket and pulled something out. "You might need this."

The redhead took the cuff key from Kendall, then unlocked and removed Sadie's cuffs. She sprang from her spot and attacked her brother. "You can't do this. I am your blood."

He knocked her back down with one blow and she hit her head against the wall. He picked the cuffs off the ground. Sadie didn't get back up again. I wasn't sure if he killed her or just knocked her unconscious.

Briggs stood in the doorway. His jaw worked back and forth while he glared at Kendall. I'd seen that look a few times before. He was angry. I had one more try. "Paul, before Carly gets the news of my death, call Rock and make him come back to town. She's going to need him."

He cast a brief glance at me before he turned and left the room.

It occurred to me that was probably the last time I would ever say Rock's name. I hadn't let it pass my lips since he ran off with Daisy, nor let anyone else speak it in front of me. And that thought made everything more real to me. I swore to myself if I somehow survived. I'd stop forbidding people—especially his own sister, Carly—from saying his name in front of me. Hell, I might even return Daisy's call. Tears sprang into my eyes then.

"You got Detective Palmer's cuffs on ya, Hanson?"

Hanson nodded.

"Cuff the girl to the bed, then go get the gasoline."

"Gasoline? What are you doing?" I knew very well what he was doing, but it's all I could think to say.

Hanson stooped down in front of us. He was the same cop talking to Rowdy at the dance. I'd seen him at the department picnic Carly had taken me to this past summer. He'd had a new baby. It stuck in my head because the baby didn't have a single bit of fuzz on his completely round head and when he cried, his face turned red. Hanson's wife was talking about how she'd eaten a ton of cherry tomatoes during her pregnancy, and now she'd given birth to her own little cherry tomato. She called him her "little mater."

"How's the little mater?" I asked. I hoped I was doing the right thing. It could go a few different ways.

His hands shook slightly. "What?"

"You don't remember me? I'm Carly's friend. We met at the picnic."

He clamped his mouth shut and grabbed my arm.

"He's what now, about five months old? Did he ever get any hair? I bet it's going to come in red like your wife's. Her name is Molly, isn't it?"

"Stop. Talking." He said through clenched teeth.

"She was sure proud of your promotion to sergeant. Would she be proud if she could see what you're doing now?"

His face clouded over, and he slammed a cuff onto my left wrist. He whispered, "I'm doing this for her. She's sick. I'm sorry. He said it's the only way I don't lose my insurance."

That's how Kendall controlled the force. He found their weaknesses and exploited them.

"You about done there, Hanson?" Briggs stood up from his chat with Sadie and walked over to us. "You make sure it's secure. If she gets loose, it's on you. You wouldn't want me to take it out on your pretty little wife and son, would you?"

Hanson squeezed the cuff so tight I thought my bones were going to crack underneath the pressure.

"She's not going anywhere, sir." Hanson stood and wiped his hands on his pants.

Briggs returned then with something in a cloth. He placed it on the floor beside Sadie, who was still unconscious from the Mayor's blow.

"Hurry up, Paul. The position of the gun doesn't matter. Just so long as it's only her fingerprints on it. This whole floor will collapse once the flames downstairs get high enough. We just need it to look like Sadie was holding these two hostage."

Briggs was the last one out of the room. He stopped and gave me a look that I couldn't quite interpret. Then said, "Remember that time you and Carly played hide and seek at my house, and I couldn't find you?"

I shook my head in confusion. "What?"

"I should've looked harder." He closed the door behind him.

chapter
thirty-three

I DIDN'T KNOW what the hell he meant. What did him not finding us in a stupid game of hide and seek decades ago have anything to do with all of this? Was it just remorse? Was he remembering us as kids and wishing he didn't have to kill Carly's best friend? A bit too late for that.

I didn't have time to consider it further because Lily reappeared then. "You've got to get out of here. They've started a fire downstairs."

"I can't." I held up my cuffed hand for emphasis.

Rowdy showed up then. "They're gone. They left Hanson on lookout, but my dad posted him at the back door in case Sadie wakes up before the fire takes her."

"How hard did he hit her? Did he kill her?" I asked.

Rowdy said, "No, she's still alive. Her chest is rising and falling."

Then she was our only hope. I needed her to wake up and go put the fire out. "Sadie! Wake up!"

"She might have a concussion. My dad hit my mom so hard once he put her in the hospital. She filed for divorce a week later and left town."

"Your dad is a real dick," I said.

"You're just now figuring that out?" Rowdy smirked. "But yeah. I don't know how Briggs ever got involved with him. He seemed like a decent guy."

"Decent isn't the word I would've used." I thought again about what he said to me as he walked out. If he was a decent person, he wouldn't have left us here. Or at the very least, he could've helped in some small way. Holy cow! That was it! I flattened myself as much as I could to try to reach under the bed. That's what he was trying to tell me.

"What are you doing?" Rowdy asked.

"Looking for the handcuff key I dropped earlier. He said something about hide and seek before he left. This one time we hid under his bed, and he couldn't find us. We hid so long he finally gave up and started grilling burgers. He must have seen the key when he was planting the gun near Sadie and that was his way of telling me where it was." I felt under the bed. Careful not to swipe so that I wouldn't knock it out of my reach. But the only thing underneath my hand was a dusty hardwood floor.

Rowdy leaned down and peered under the bed. "I see

it! Move your hand a bit to the right. Now a little forward. Further."

"That's as far as I can reach."

"Keep trying. You are like a millimeter from it. There!"

I had the cuff key between my fingers.

"You have to hurry," Lily hollered. "The fire is spreading quickly."

I stared at the key—which was more like a pin—in my palm. "How does this thing work?"

Rowdy walked me through it and by the time I got my hand free, I could smell the smoke.

"Dusty, wake up. We're getting out of here."

He was as pale as the moon. But he opened his eyes. "Hey," he said. Then closed them again.

"Wake up." I lightly slapped his cheeks.

His eyes fluttered open again briefly. "I'm just gonna rest."

"No, you're not. I'm sorry about this." I dug my fingers into his shoulder and his eyes flew open.

He let out a string of expletives. "Why did you do that?"

"The house is on fire, and we have to get out of here."

"Hanson is still outside the back door. You're going to have to sneak past him somehow and get out the front," Coach Abbott said.

I didn't even know how we were going to make it to

the stairs. Much less *down* them. And we were supposed to do all of this without Hanson hearing us? Despair suddenly hit me.

"And if you can't do it quietly, you have a gun." He cocked his head toward Sadie.

"And what are the chances that's loaded?"

"You said Briggs put it there. So maybe he left a round in the chamber for you as well?"

Doubtful, but I was grappling for any infinitesimal chance I could of us surviving this. First, I had to try to stand. Pain shot through my leg, and I felt faint with the intensity of it. I collapsed onto the bed, and the room started closing in.

"Stay with me, Star." Palmer said.

"I'm here. Just give me a minute."

"I don't think we have a minute." He coughed. The smoke was wafting upstairs now.

I hurled myself across the bed to reach the other side, where Sadie lay on the floor. I felt like I was going to pass out from the pain, but I held it together. I reached for the gun. No time to check whether or not it was loaded. I would just have to hope. But I'd rather die instantly by Hanson's gun than burn to death up here. I rolled back over on the mattress and pushed myself up, shoved the gun in my waistband, and found Dusty leaning against the wall with his eyes closed. Blood soaked his shirt.

He held out a hand. "You ready to go?"

I nodded. I couldn't tell you which of us was leaning on the other. But maybe we were like an arch, both supporting the other. I tried to put weight on the leg that Briggs shot, and it buckled underneath me. My fall caused Dusty to lose his balance, and he tumbled down as well.

I closed my eyes. I was so tired. We were never going to get out of here.

"You're not giving up that easily, Star!" I opened my eyes to find Coach Abbott standing over me with his hands on his hips, looking every bit the coach he was. "Now get back up and try again!"

"I can't."

Lily stood beside him. "Star, I know it's hard. I know you're in pain, and you feel you can't go another inch, but Dusty needs you."

I rolled my head over to look at him and he lay there with his eyes closed, breathing shallowly. I don't know how I didn't see it before, but he and Lily had the same kind eyes. He and Carly were the only good cops Dead End had left. I couldn't leave Carly out there to battle it out alone. I sat up, fighting the dizziness that threatened to overtake me. "Come on, Dusty. We're getting out of here."

He pressed his lips together and nodded. He pushed himself up and wobbled a moment, then steadied himself and reached for my hand. When we got to the stairs, the smoke was so thick, we could barely see. I took a step down and the bad leg nearly buckled under me. Dusty caught my arm. "Sit down on your butt and slide down that way, step by step."

I did as he said, and he sidled past me and gripped the handrail.

"Cover your mouth with this." He removed his shirt and tossed it to me. "And hand me the gun. I'm going on ahead to take care of Hanson."

He slid out the clip, swore, then shoved it back in again and continued down the stairs mumbling, "I guess I'm gonna have to do this the hard way."

He made it to the bottom and looked back at me and smiled, then whispered, "Is my mom still here?"

"Yes." I couldn't see anything, but I doubted she would leave now, and he seemed to need her to be here.

"Tell her...whatever happens to me, she better not ever tell you the story of the time I ruined her best pair of heels." He winked and disappeared around the corner.

I kept making my way down on my butt, step by step, and was halfway down the stairs when I heard a gunshot. I jumped up in response, forgetting about my leg. All I could think of was Dusty needed me. I lost my balance and toppled forward. I reached for something to grab, but I caught only air. I heard a crunch when I hit my head, and everything went black.

. . .

I felt no pain, but it was dark again. I tried to follow the voices but felt like I was trying to walk through jelly. A small sliver of light appeared in the dark and suddenly the voices grew louder, then the light grew brighter, and I blinked.

"You're awake," Teeny said and gripped my hand. I hadn't heard that much joy in her voice since she'd finally beat me in Mario Kart for the first time last year.

I tried to speak, but my mouth felt like cotton.

I turned my head to the side and found her with tears shining in her eyes. Aunt Mer stood behind her and Uncle Gavin stood close by with similar expressions. "How are you feeling?"

I thought about that for a moment. I didn't hurt anywhere. But all the tubes and the bags hanging on the pole next to the bed were probably the cause of that. I opened my mouth again to speak, and it took me a couple of tries, but I said, "Palmer?"

Aunt Mer patted my shoulder. "He saved your life, honey. He pulled you out of the burning cabin."

So many thoughts swirled through my head. I'd heard the gunshot. How did he pull me out? But the more important thing was what they were not saying. "Where is he?"

"He's in the ICU, honey, but he's stable."

Relief filled me.

I heard the low roar of voices again and once my eyes

came into focus, I found Aunt Willa Jo standing behind Granny's scooter at the foot of the bed, and out in the hall I could hear what sounded like the rest of my family.

"Remind me when you're out of here to yell at you for going out to the cabin by yourself." Granny said and tried to give me her stern look, but instead her face scrunched up and she scrubbed at her eyes. "You could've died, honey."

"How am I not dead? I fell down the stairs. I heard something crack."

"You have a concussion, but the doctor seems to think you'll make a full recovery. And you'll have an awful scar on your leg from the bullet." Aunt Mer said.

"Briggs?" I croaked out.

"He's still out there. Carly is out looking for him. Kendall is in custody. I know this is a lot of information right now, honey. Why don't you just rest? Now that we know you're okay, I can herd most of the family out of here so you can have some peace and quiet."

"Yeah, you have to be all better by your birthday," Teeny said.

My birthday. Halloween.

"Honey, Let's see if Star is out of the hospital by then."

"If not, we can bring the party to her."

I smiled. It was good to see Teeny a bit back to herself

again. Movement at the door caught my eye then, and Zeke stood there with his hands in his pockets.

He was Teeny's father.

She didn't know yet. What would she do when she found out that the man she'd always known as her best friend's cool dad was her own biological father? And how would Kira feel having to share her dad with her best friend? I could almost see those thoughts going through Zeke's own head. I wanted to reassure him we'd tell her together. Soon. But that would have to wait. Instead, I gave him a small wave and a smile.

Teeny turned and dashed to Zeke and grabbed his hand. "Get in here. You're part of the family, too. Where's Kira?"

"She's with her mom. Jessi-Lyn didn't want to be alone, but they both send their love."

Jessi-Lyn sending her love to me? A week ago, I couldn't have even imagined it.

"Oh, and Jess says to tell you the green Jello is to be avoided at all costs." A small smile played across his lips. "Make sure they bring you the yellow one."

I smiled and surveyed the room, taking in the sight of all my relatives milling about. Both blood and found. When Mamma left me and Astra here all those years ago, I thought we were being punished. But now I could see what she'd given us instead was the greatest gift of all. A family.

epilogue

Halloween

I stabbed my fork into the giant slice of birthday cake in front of me. I was stuffed from the big spread we'd just had, which included Zeke's nachos and all the other family favorites, but there's always room for cake.

Aunt Willa Jo clinked her fork on her glass and said, "Can I say something?"

"Yes, you may, *Madame Mayor*," Holly said.

Aunt Willa Jo shook her head. "Don't jump the gun on that just yet. Just because my opponent is in jail awaiting trial doesn't mean I'm in by default. Someone on the city council may decide to run now that they don't have to go up against Kendall."

"Can we quit talking about the election stuff and just

get to the presents," Kira asked. "Teeny and I got Star the perfect gift."

"Yes, you've mentioned that a time or two," Aunt Willa Jo said. "All I was going to say is, I am so thankful for every single one of you, especially since we've lost Aunt Tatty so recently."

Lost is one way to put it. She disappeared, leaving only a note that she wanted to see Europe before she died. How in the world she was going to manage that by herself was beyond me. Everyone had been in an uproar about it. Except Granny. She'd acted like it was the most normal thing a woman in her nineties could do. She had Kira and Teeny take some big trash bags down to the dumpster shortly after Aunt Tatty left, and one fell open and some clothes spilled out. I recognized Tatty's favorite sweater.

"I am thankful for all of you as well," said Kira. "Now can we do the present?"

Aunt Mer said, "Okay then, reveal your big surprise. It better not be a puppy!"

Teeny giggled and for a horrified moment, I thought she had gotten me a puppy. I was much more a kitten girl myself. But then Kira swept her arm toward the door and said, "Okay, without further ado..."

Just as the doors opened, Teeny drew her finger across her neck in the universal symbol that meant stop. Or sometimes, "You're dead," but this was most likely the first one.

Oh, good grief, can she not get it together?" Kira asked.

Palmer hobbled through and found us all quietly staring at him.

"He is not your present. Everyone mingle while we get this sorted out," Kira said.

I laughed and rolled myself toward Palmer. "You look much better than the last time I saw you."

"So do you, and you have some fancy wheels." He nodded to the wheelchair Teeny and Kira had decorated for me with ghosts, witches, and pumpkins. "What was that about me being your present?"

"Evidently, Kira and Teeny have come up with some super awesome, spectacularly amazing—their words not mine—present for me. And it was supposed to be delivered just now, but apparently there was some sort of snafu."

He ran a hand through his hair. "Well, I am not much of a present, but I do have a present for you."

I took the small flat package wrapped in black tissue from his hand. I ran a finger over the purple, sparkly, miniature witch hats dotting the paper.

"You can open it now if you want. Or wait until—"

I'd had the tissue ripped off before he finished his sentence. I gasped. It was an old well-worn but in decent condition blue covered copy of *The Secret in the Old Clock*.

"It's not a first edition Nancy Drew or anything. But I thought you might like it."

"I adore it. And even better that you got her name right." I grinned.

"It's printed inside the book, so..." He smiled.

"Thank you. You didn't have to get me anything. It's present enough seeing you up on two feet. When you walked out that door, I thought that's the last time I'd see you. You were like the hero in an action flick. I didn't want to bug you about it in the hospital while you were healing, but I've gotta know. How did you overtake Hanson?"

He ducked his head. "The idiot was taking a leak. I snuck up behind him, intending to hold the empty gun to his head, but he turned around at the last moment, in mid-stream, and uh...sprayed me."

"Holy crap!" I tried to stifle a giggle.

Color filled his face. "Yeah, but I held the gun on him, and he pulled his own and called my bluff. I squeezed the trigger, and the gun discharged, and I shot him in the neck. The clip was empty, but there'd been a round in the chamber."

"Briggs."

"Yeah, he helped us twice that day."

"Three times. He was also the one who called the fire department, according to Carly."

"How's she doing? She's not here, is she?" He glanced around the room.

I shook my head, and a lump formed in my throat. She felt horrible for missing my fortieth birthday. But after hunting Briggs down and convincing him to let her take him in, she wasn't doing so great. It didn't feel quite right celebrating my birthday without her, especially when she was grieving, but there was no way Teeny and Kira were going to let me postpone my party.

"Do you have any news on...the crime scene? Have the Rangers...?" I couldn't finish that sentence. But after talking to Granny about the mojo bag, we had theories about why Astra was invisible to me. The spell was for hiding things. Astra had Aunt Tatty make it so that she could hide her relationship with Zeke, but Sadie used it to keep Astra's body from being discovered.

"They haven't found the well yet. Sadie had it filled in and Kendall is claiming to know nothing about it," Palmer said.

A pang of guilt hit me then. We hadn't left Sadie behind on purpose. The firefighters said they found Palmer and I collapsed together in a heap a few feet from the house and it was burning so hot they couldn't get in.

"Thank you. For getting us out of there."

"Me? Star, you never gave up. Even after we both fell. I thought that was it. We were going to die there. But you somehow gathered your last bit of energy and made me get up."

"It wasn't me. It was the ghosts. And your mom. She told me you needed me to get you out of there."

A sad smile crossed his face. "Is she here now?"

I nodded and took the glass of sparkling grape juice Kira shoved into my hand just then. "She's sitting on the bar, swinging her legs to the music."

"Sounds about right." Palmer took a glass as well and clinked his flute against mine.

"She promised to tell me about the heels someday. She said something about a sequined dress as well?"

"Now you're just making stuff up."

I laughed and was about to give him a witty retort, but Kira's voice rang out then.

"Everyone, she's here. The present is here."

Oh God, it must be a puppy. And a female one at that. I knew nothing about raising a puppy! All the pee pads and hyper-activeness. How was I gonna break their hearts when I refused the gift?

The door swung open then and a blonde in cut-offs, pink boots, and rhinestone covered shades waltzed in. Not a puppy. Not a puppy at all.

"The party has arrived!" Daisy shimmied her hips, then strode over to me, took my drink from my hand, and downed it. "Drink up, witches!"

The End

Thank you so much for reading the first book in the Dead-End Witches series, which is also my debut novel. If you got all the way to the end, you've made a 1970s little girl's dream come true!

For all the latest news and a sneak peek of Book 2, sign up for my newsletter HERE.

afterword

Dear Reader,

I keep trying to delete this section because I feel like I'm rambling, but anyone who knows me well has heard me ramble more than once. And since this is (hopefully) the beginning of a long relationship, it's best you know what to expect from me from the start.

So here you go. The real me.

I cannot freaking believe I finally finished a book! I mean...I finished another book a few years ago...but then I accidentally unfinished it and am not quite sure how to actually refinish it...but that is another story for another time, and hopefully you will eventually get to meet Grace and Charlie. But holy crap, y'all...a book! A real. Live. Book.

Trying to breathe and type at the same time and remember not to curse...that's my real talent. ;)

This book only took me three years and can I tell you I am so proud of myself for that progress I could explode into a cloud of glitter. But I won't because that is quite messy and hard to clean up.

I adore these characters. I wasn't so sure about them at first because I had spent 16 years getting to know Grace and Charlie (from the finished but unraveled book) and then Star pops up and I'm like uh, who are you?

At first she told me she lived far away from Dead End and got a call to come home because Carly's body had been found. Then all of a sudden she changes it to already living in Dead End and Zeke shows up all ghost-like in the graveyard where she is hanging out with Astra and Lizzy. (Who is Lizzy, you ask?! Right?! What the heck did you do with Lizzy, Star?!)

Also at one point, Star had red hair and perfect eyebrows and she grew and shrunk from between 5 feet 6 and 6 feet tall. Like, Star, make up your mind already about who you are. So you see my problem. I didn't know her like I knew Grace. I am still learning who she is, but that is the fun of playing with your imaginary friends. Right?!

And Palmer...I wasn't so sure I liked him at all, and planned to kill him off until an early reader got all swoony over the chemistry between him and Star and I was like... what chemistry? Star kept this from me.

Someone also wanted me to axe Aunt Merileee, who

keeps changing the spelling of her own name, so if you see it as Merrilee in there accidentally, that's not my fault. It's Aunt Mer's. And maybe she did that because I did try to remove her from existence. But couldn't quite bring myself to it. She might feel useless in this book (Sorry, Mer) but she has a purpose. I know she will eventually reveal it to me.

Oh and Granny....holy cow, the secrets she has. I CANNOT WAIT to tell y'all those. Like I am so giddy right now I am forgetting to breathe again!

But y'all, I am so excited to bring you this series. And I really hope you stick around and give this author a chance. I am sure I made mistakes and there are some snooty Rudys (sorry to any non-snooty Rudys for slandering your collective name) out there saying, "What kind of person can't remember if their character's name has one R or two!" Hey, it's hard keeping all the voices in my head organized. ;)

But for you, yes YOU in the shirt over there. The one who is sticking around and who loves these characters and this story just as much as I do. YOU are the one this book is for! I bet you laughed in all the right places, and didn't throw the book across the room even once!

You are my hero, and I thank you heartily for your dollars, your time, your adoration, and your review. That last one is a wish instead of a given. :)

Also, if you sign up for my newsletter (It's a ghost

town in there right now because...baby author, remember?) I promise to give you the real me all the time. Who knows what I will talk about, but I promise not to be one of those people who are like "buy my book, buy my book, here's my book, buy it already..."

No sirree, Bobbert!

I will give you cool things like photos of my Scottish Fold cats. One of whom sits up like a human and lets me put stuff in her lap like my hot pink PS5 controller. A first look at every new tarot deck I buy. As well as behind the scenes stuff like what happened after Daisy said, "Drink Up, Witches!" Did Star run her over in her wheel chair? Or did she throw her birthday present from Palmer at her?

But if you really don't need anything else (even something as amazing as my wordy words) cluttering up your inbox, you can always find me on Instagram @authorlesliegail.

Okay, I have rambled enough, but in all seriousness, thank you so much for buying this book! You are a freaking rockstar! Love ya, bye!

Love and Magic,
Leslie

acknowledgments

This is one of the fun parts! How many times have I read the acknowledgements in other authors' books and mentally composed my own in my head?!

I know I am going to forget to mention someone by name, so my deepest apologies in advance. But thank you to all of you who've been with me on this wild ride!

The thing is, the journey didn't start with just this book. When I was seven, I wrote ridiculously dumb stories that my mother thought was "precious." She took them to work and shared them with her coworkers. They decided it would be fun to publish them on the company copy machine and sell them in the break room for fifty cents each. When my mother brought home that first handful of change, I was hooked. So first, I'd like to thank Gayle Sharp, Kathy Bramlett, and LaRae Clark for encouraging that little girl. And of course, my amazing Mumsie for bringing me into this world, loving me every minute of my life...especially between the ages of 16 and 22, and for always believing in me!

Thank you to my entire family for encouraging me over the years for everything from my poems as a teen to my goofy emails from Sweden as an adult. Plus, a special shout-out to Lala for my message in a bottle. I never gave up, Sissy!

Thank you to my Swedish family for always understanding when I brought my laptop with me during the summer and for asking all the right questions about my book.

To my Oceans Six crew: Scarlett, Celia, Kristin, Brittany, and Alli. We began as strangers at a conference back in 2015, but I couldn't imagine my life without you all now. Thank you for the questions that challenged me in Reno, the Hurricanes that sustained me in New Orleans, Tarot and late-night walks to Wisconsin from Stillwater, Mexican food and Buffy episodes in Austin, and all the Zoom calls and virtual writing retreats that kept me sane in between! Additional thanks to both Celia and Brittany for reading an earlier draft of this book and for encouraging me to not give up.

Thank you to Stacey Kade for helping me get my first book ready to pitch back in 2018. I know that first draft was awful, and I apologize profusely to your eyeballs, but you did a lovely job of being both encouraging and educational.

Huge thanks to my Pitch Wars mentor, Susan Bishop Crispell, for an amazing experience. You showed me I could do hard things in a short amount of time. Your words, "I wouldn't have chosen you if I didn't think you could do it" will forever live in my head. That one sentence sustained me long after PitchWars was over. And your continued cheerleading and support mean the world to me

And speaking of PitchWars, I want to thank both Team Mayo and Team Hell Nomayo for being in the trenches with me through PitchWars and those crazy months beyond. You all have a special place in my heart! All my love to Alexis, Elvin, Chad, Jen, Jessica, Jacki, Lyssa, Nanci, Marisa, Mary, Meg, Meryl, Susan, Rochelle, Rosie, and Ruby!

To everyone at the Better-Faster Academy who was part of this journey. All the way from Terry Schott who was my first coach at the BFA and got me excited about Strengths, to Susan Bischoff who helped me to see that I might need therapy for my Empathy (I did!), and to the rest who eventually became my coworkers and who support and cheer me on every day!

Massive thanks to Becca Syme for wanting everyone to be okay and for creating the Better-Faster Academy and teaching the writing community to *Question the Premise*. Thank you for all you've taught me these past three years. I could write a whole book on how I have changed since Traci Andrighetti (and thank you, Traci!) first pointed me in your direction back in April 2020. I wouldn't be writing these words right now if I hadn't found the BFA!

Thank you to Annette Cooke for challenging me to "finish the damn thing" by September 6th. I didn't quite make that date, but you lit a fire under me, and I got close!

To Patti Brown for Wordy Wednesdays (I just now christened it as that ha!) and for your constant encouragement and accountability. And for your gentle questions that challenge me to think a little more on something I was sure of.

Thank you to Betsie for reading this book while in London! Best Beta Ever!

Thank you, Alex, for the light you've brought to my life for over 26 years. And to Paigey for making that light brighter. I'm so proud of you both!

And to my love. My Wraith. My Tor. No single person in the known universe has been more supportive of this dream than you have been. Way back in the late 90s/early 2000s, when we were reading those "vampire books" and you said, "Hey, she writes like you." It wasn't, "You write like this famous author." And maybe it was just your Swenglish at the time, but it gave me the confidence that I was good enough to become an author too! And it only took a couple of decades! But not once did you ever suggest I should give up my dream. Thank you for always treating my writing as a career and for talking me out of quitting, more than once. Infinity.

about the author

Leslie Gail's debut novel first hit the market in 1979 with her riveting three-page illustrated novel, *The "Chrismas" Book*. It was not only a financial success—earning her a total of $2.50—it was also critically acclaimed by all the ladies in her mother's break-room group.

These days Leslie's books are slightly wordier and no longer illustrated—which is probably for the best since she never could draw a proper "babby" Jesus. And are filled with magic, mystery, and big Southern families.

Leslie lives in Austin, Texas and is proudly doing her part to Keep It Weird. When she's not plotting murder, or working the day job, you might find her removing cat hair from every surface in her house, playing board games with her husband*, enjoying Saturday Brunch and bookstores with her family, singing along loudly to Disney songs**, or haunting local graveyards wherever she travels.

*Swedish husband. He wanted to make sure y'all knew his nationality. 😉 In case you mistakenly conjured up an image of Matthew McConaughey at a Longhorns game.

The cats wanted to make sure you knew Leslie cannot sing and that they've made more pleasant sounds while coughing up hairballs.*

***Leslie wants you to know that at least her singing never ruins the handmade Swedish rugs. So there!

coming soon!

The Drama of Death, book 2 in The Dead End Witches series.